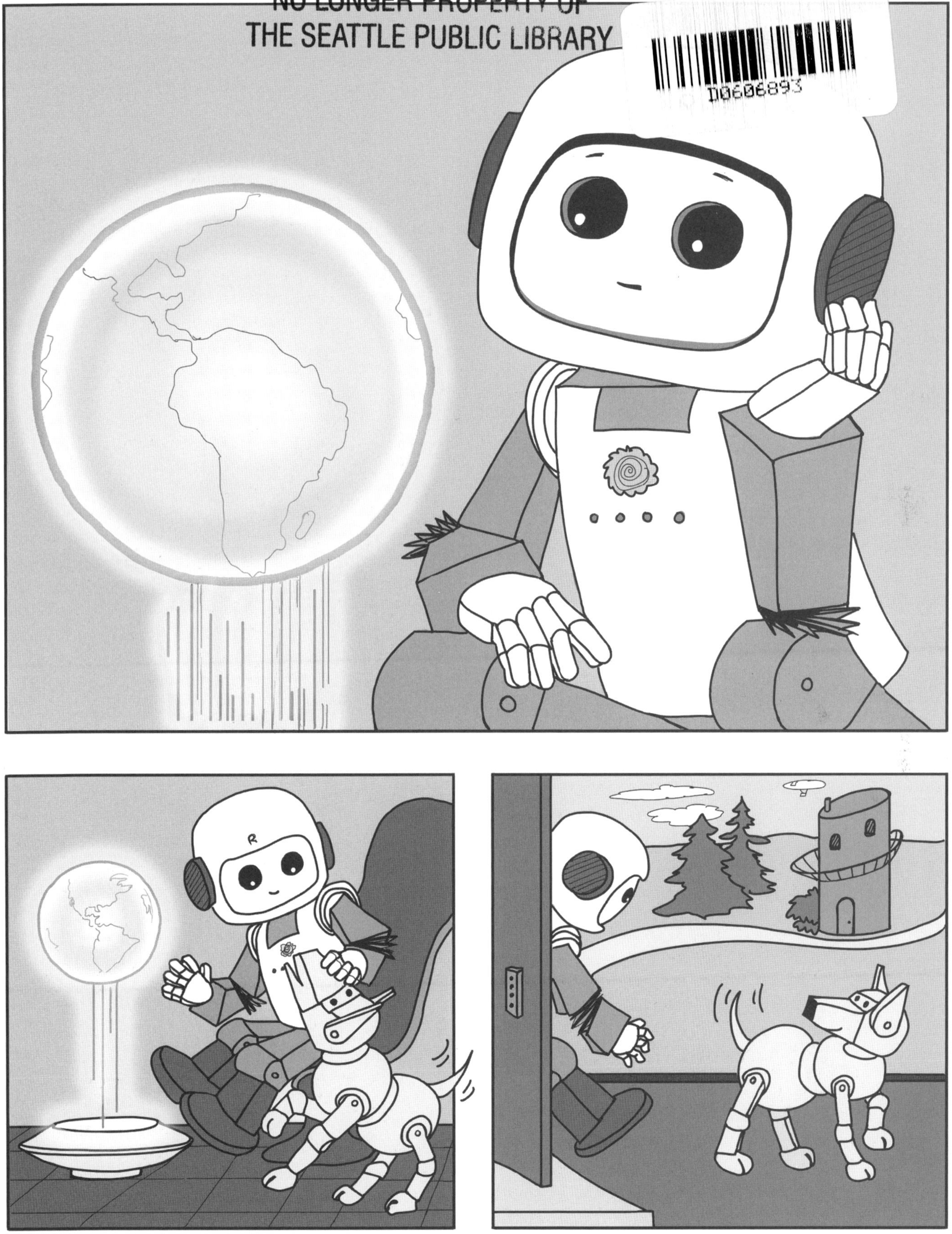

# THE ADVENTURES OF ROBO-KID

THE ADVENTURES OF
ROBO-KID

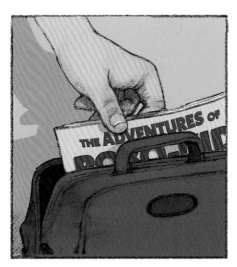

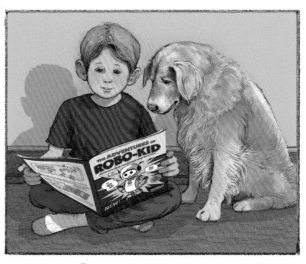

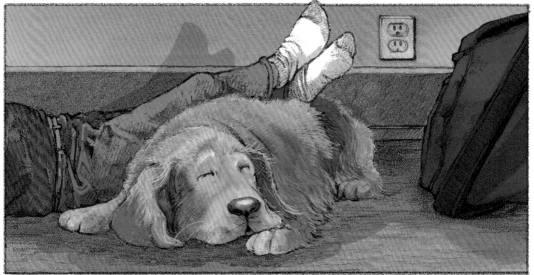

**Diane deGroat**

NEAL PORTER BOOKS
HOLIDAY HOUSE / NEW YORK

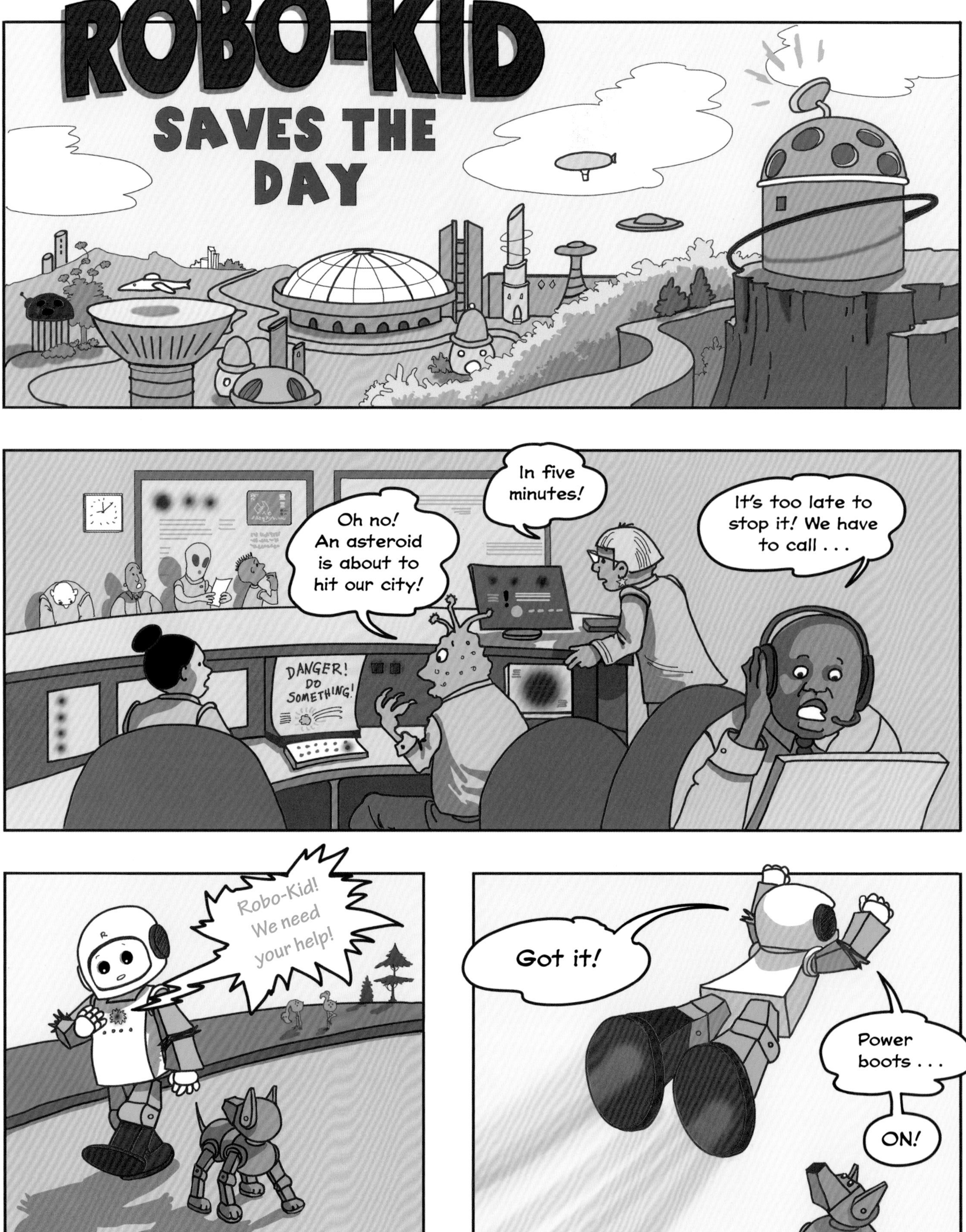
ROBO-KID
SAVES THE DAY
Oh no! An asteroid is about to hit our city!
In five minutes!
DANGER! DO SOMETHING!
It's too late to stop it! We have to call . . .
Robo-Kid! We need your help!
Got it!
Power boots . . .
ON!

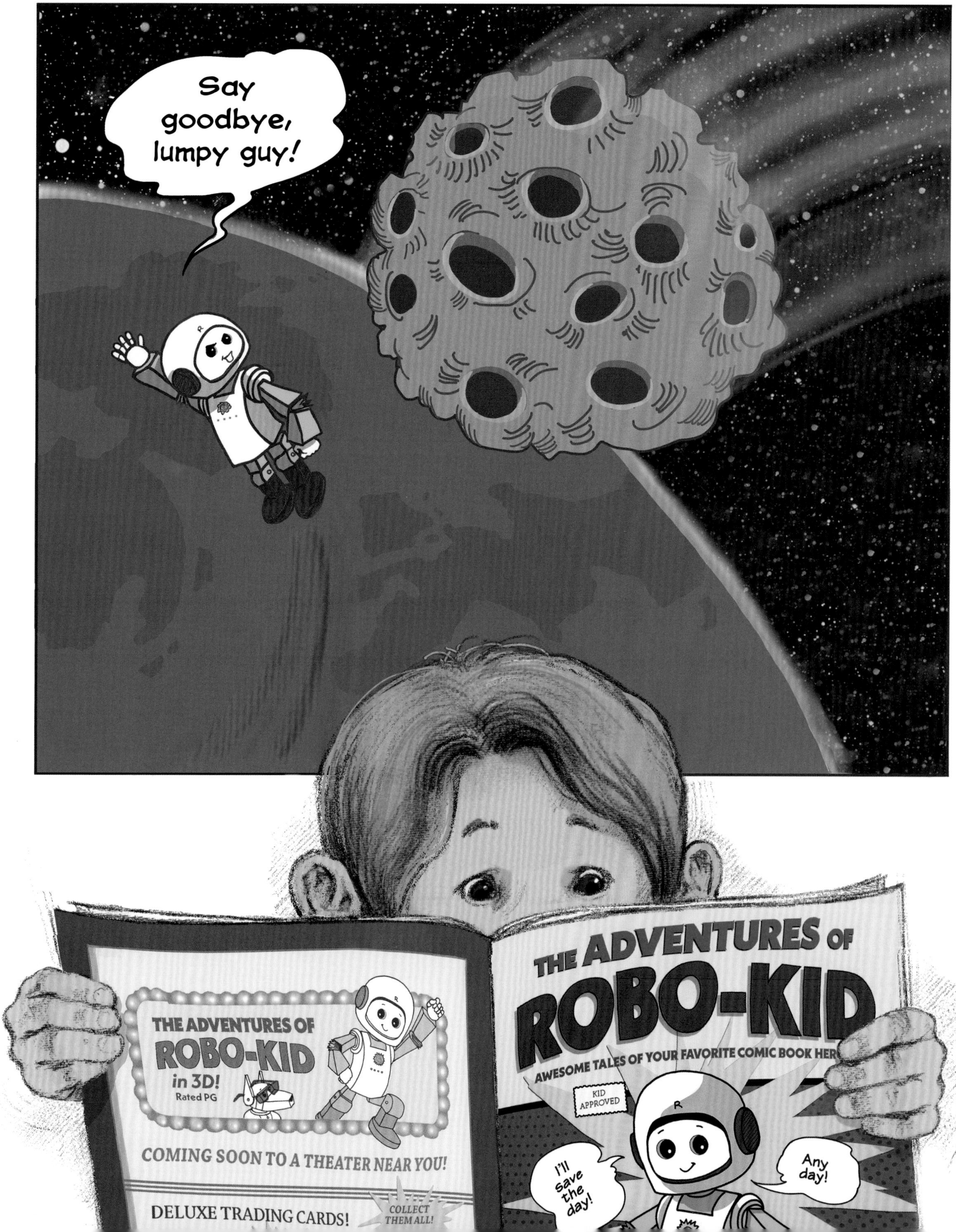

Say goodbye, lumpy guy!
THE ADVENTURES OF ROBO-KID in 3D! Rated PG
COMING SOON TO A THEATER NEAR YOU!
DELUXE TRADING CARDS!
COLLECT THEM ALL!
THE ADVENTURES OF ROBO-KID
AWESOME TALES OF YOUR FAVORITE COMIC BOOK HER
KID APPROVED
I'll save the day!
Any day!

"Ready for your swimming lesson, Henry?"

"In a minute—almost done."

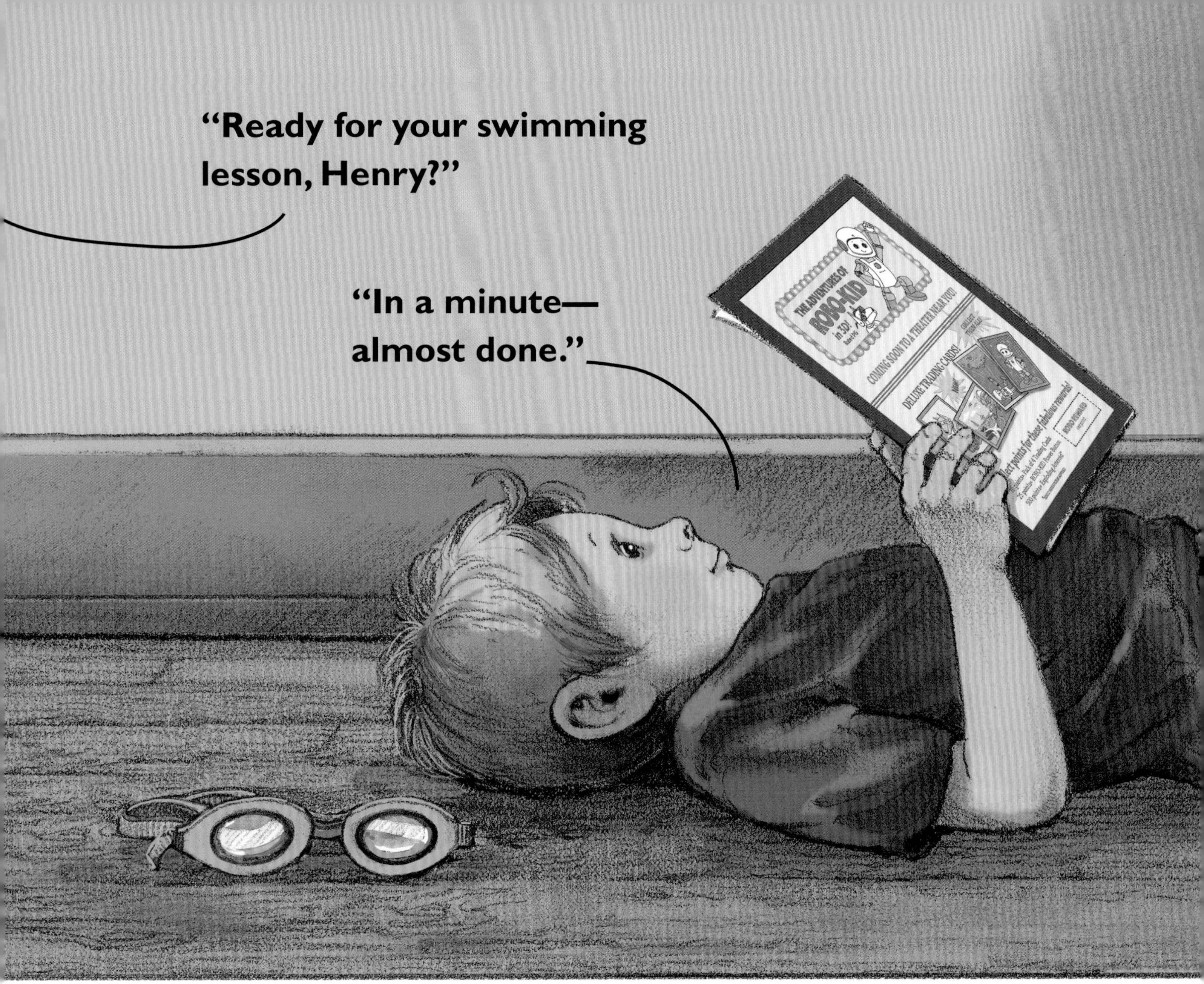
THE ADVENTURES OF ROBO-KID in 3D!
COMING SOON TO A THEATER NEAR YOU!
DELUXE TRADING CARDS!

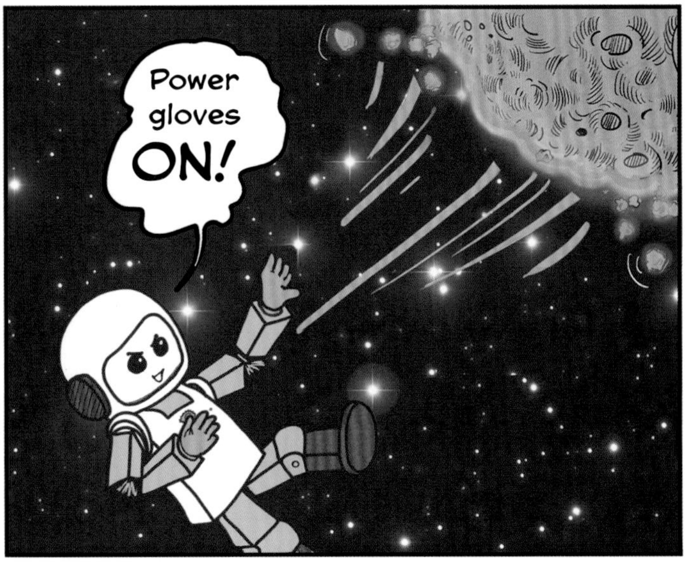
Power gloves ON!

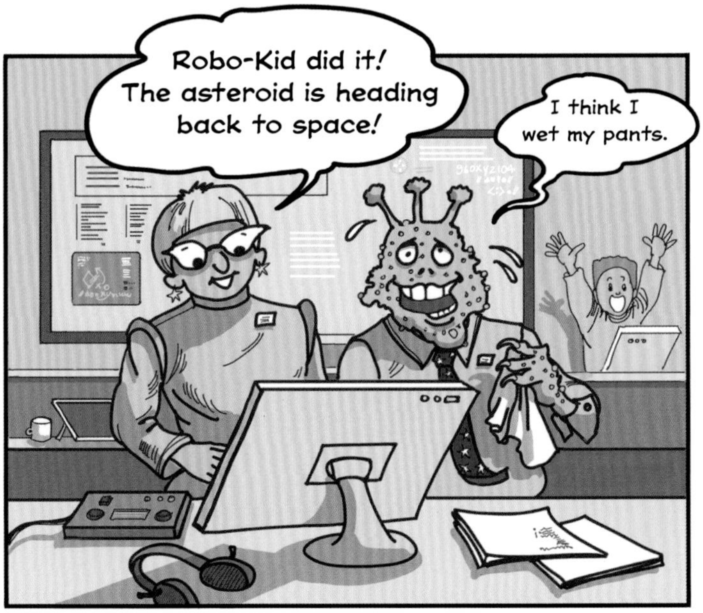
Robo-Kid did it! The asteroid is heading back to space!
I think I wet my pants.

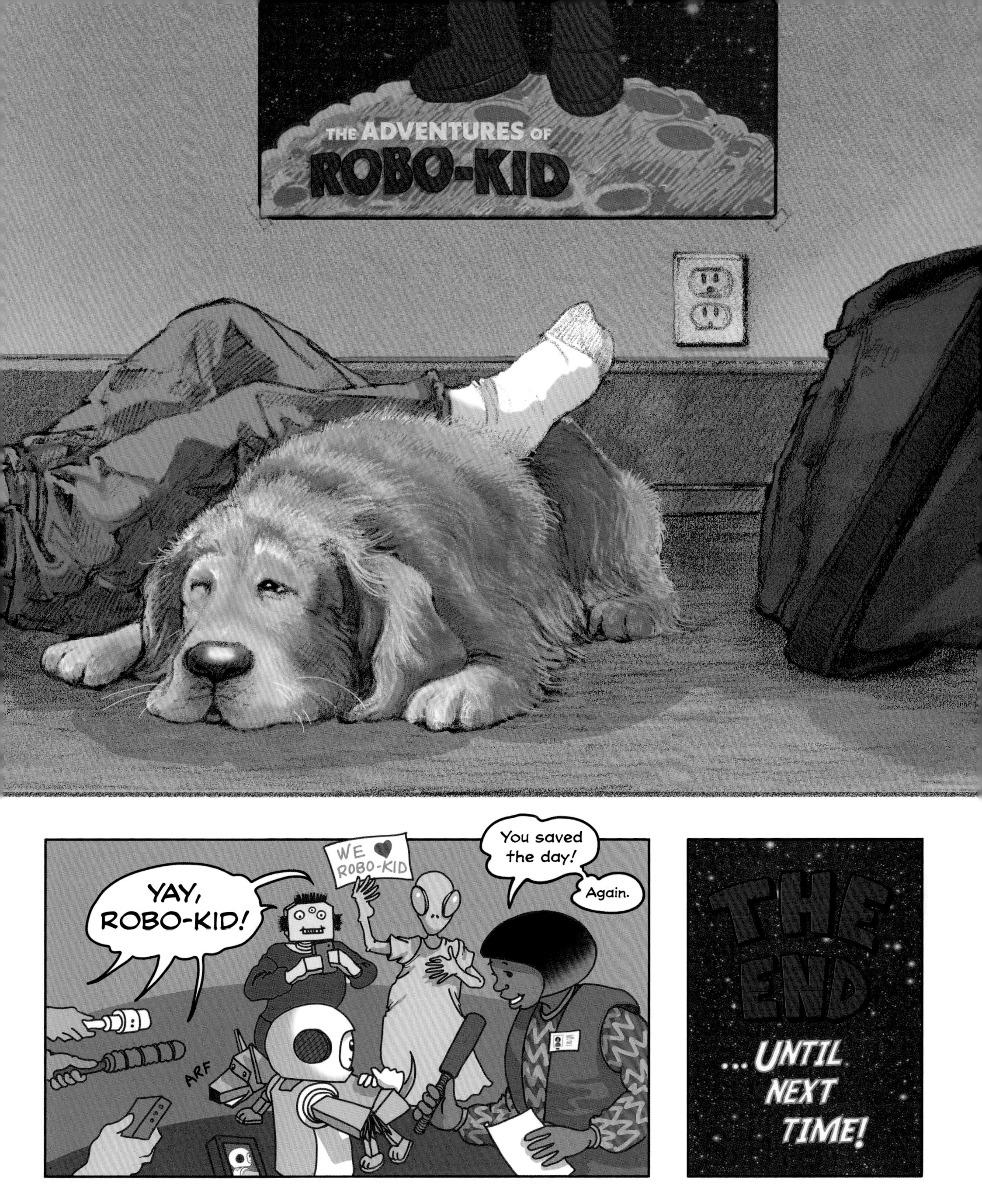
THE ADVENTURES OF ROBO-KID
YAY, ROBO-KID!
WE ♥ ROBO-KID
You saved the day!
Again.
ARF
THE END
...UNTIL NEXT TIME!

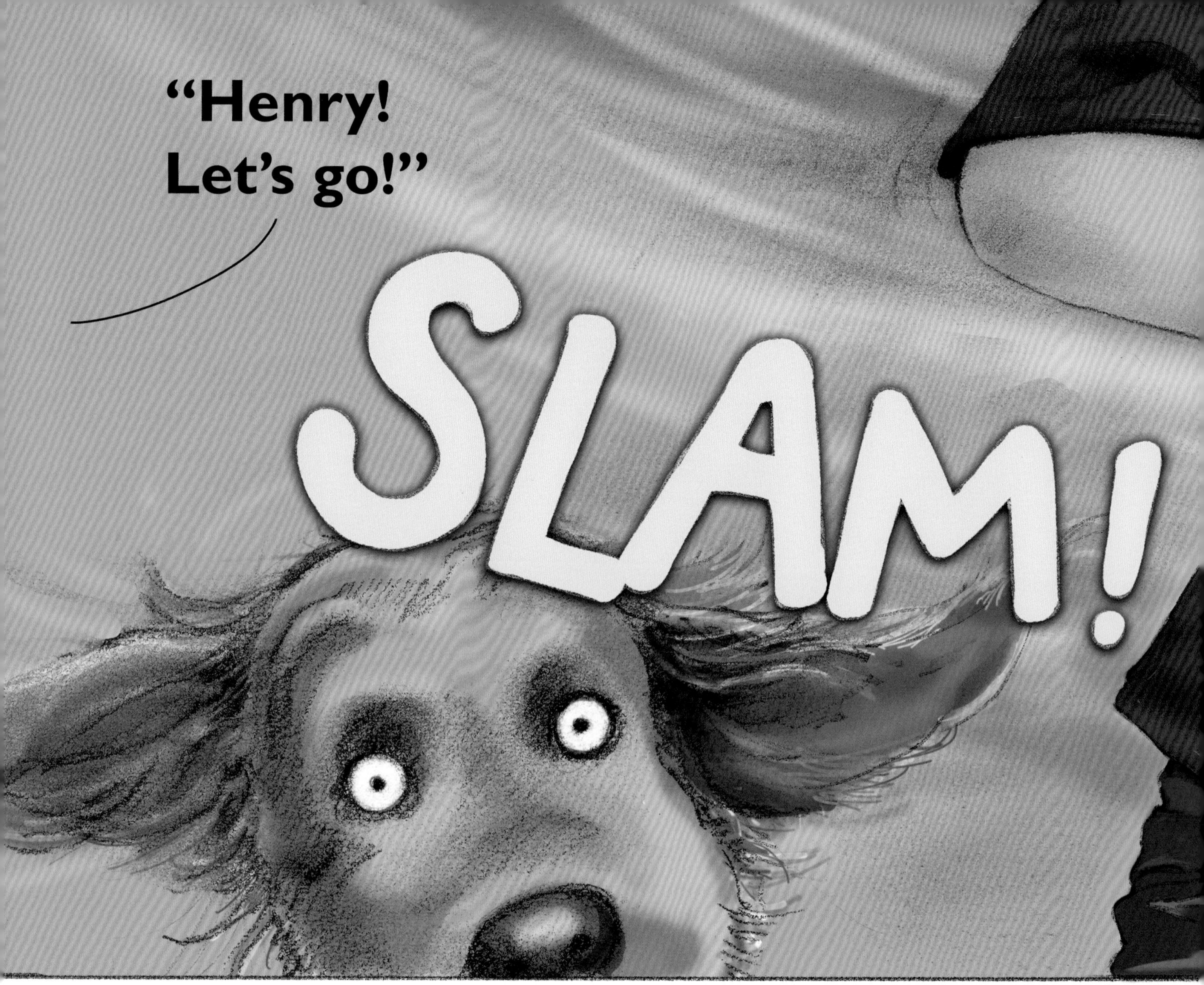
"Henry!
Let's go!"
SLAM!

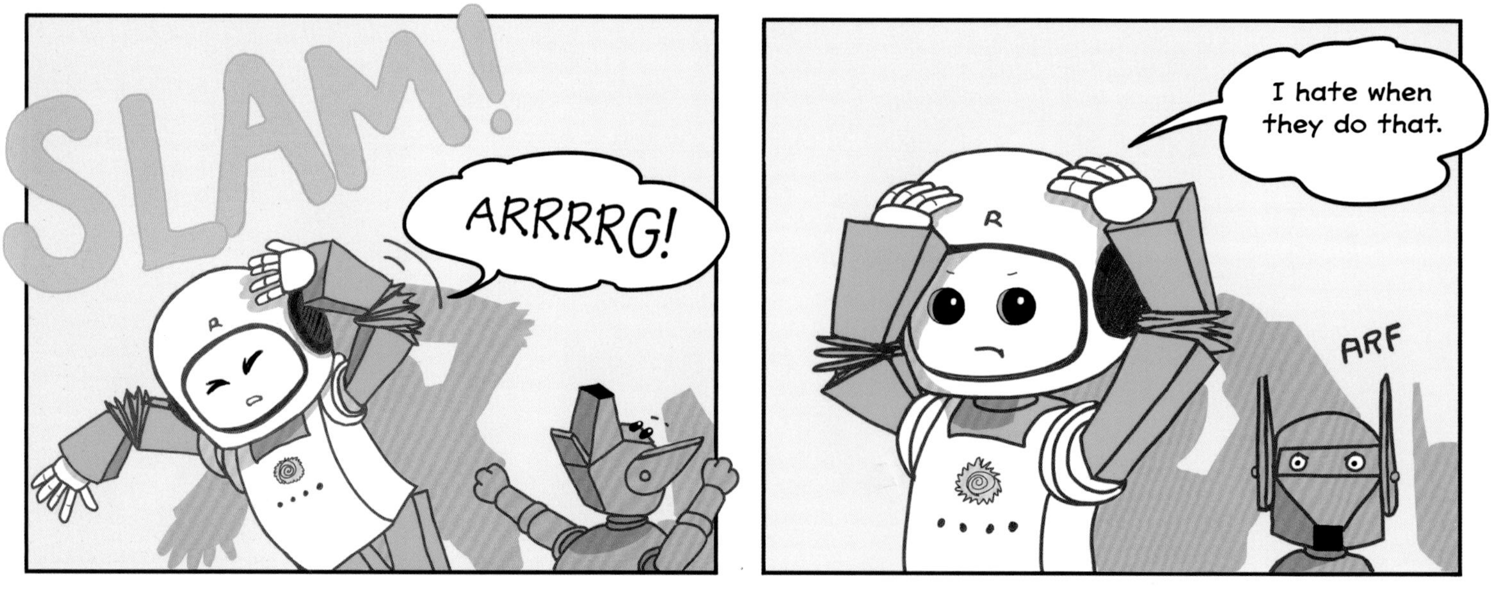
SLAM!
ARRRRG!
I hate when they do that.
ARF

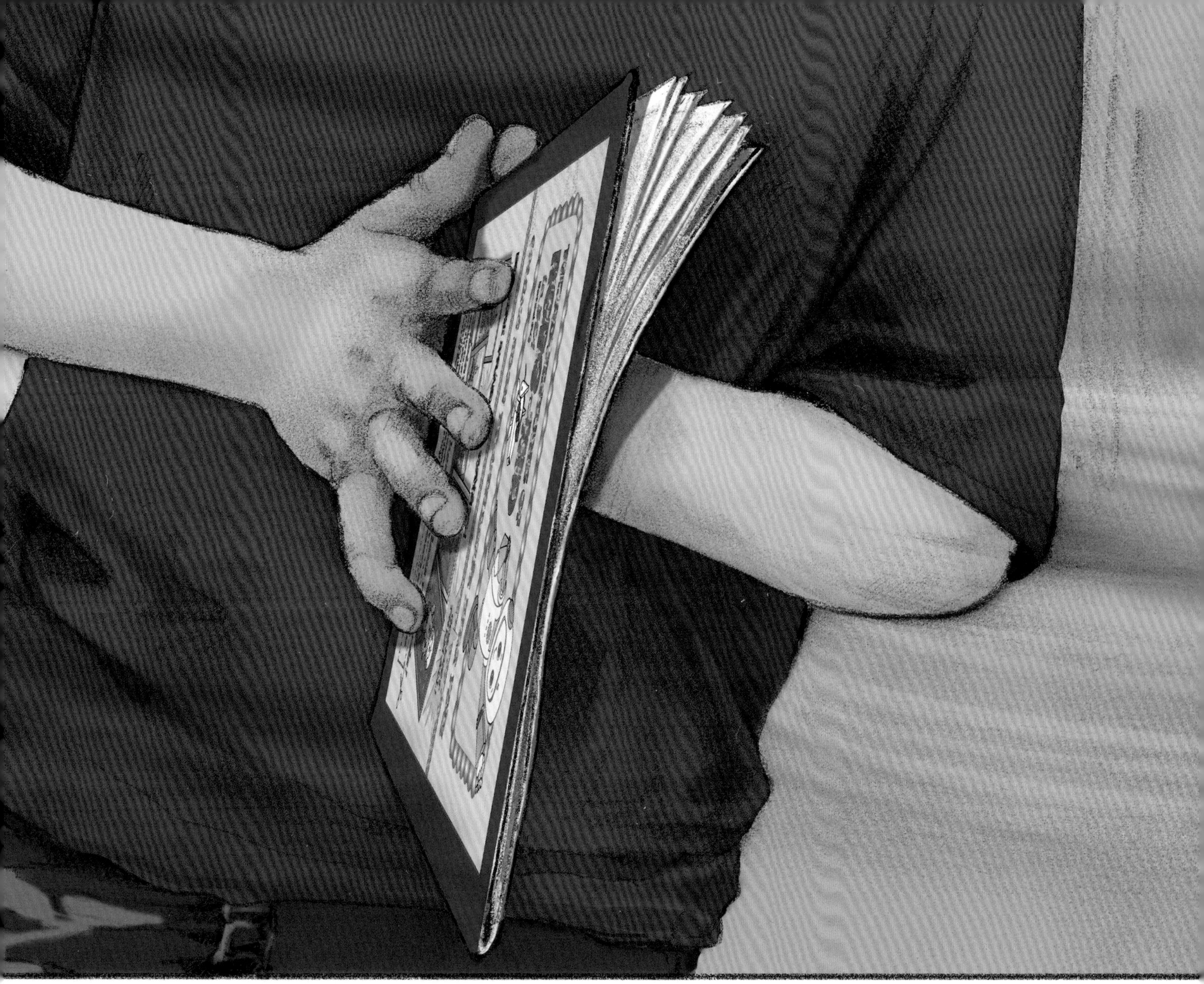

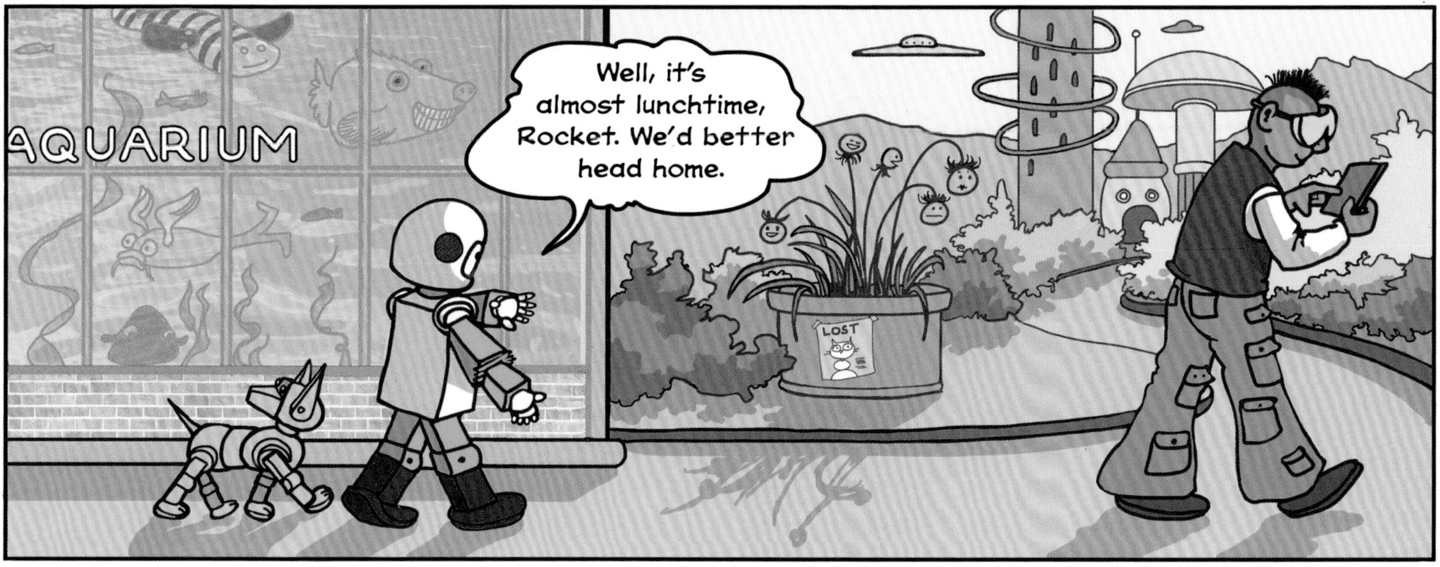
AQUARIUM
Well, it's almost lunchtime, Rocket. We'd better head home.
LOST

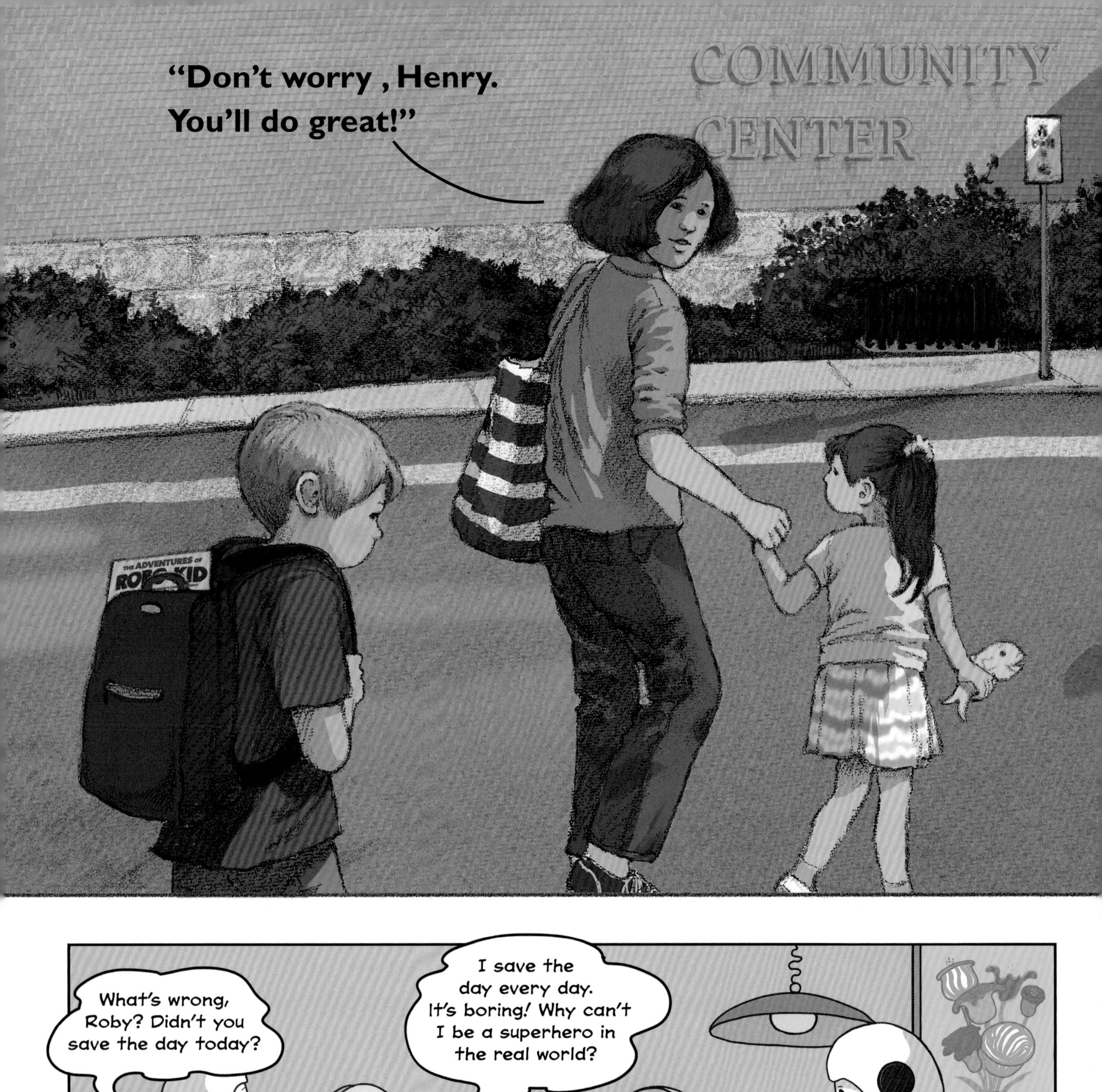
"Don't worry, Henry.
You'll do great!"
COMMUNITY
CENTER
THE ADVENTURES OF
ROBO KID

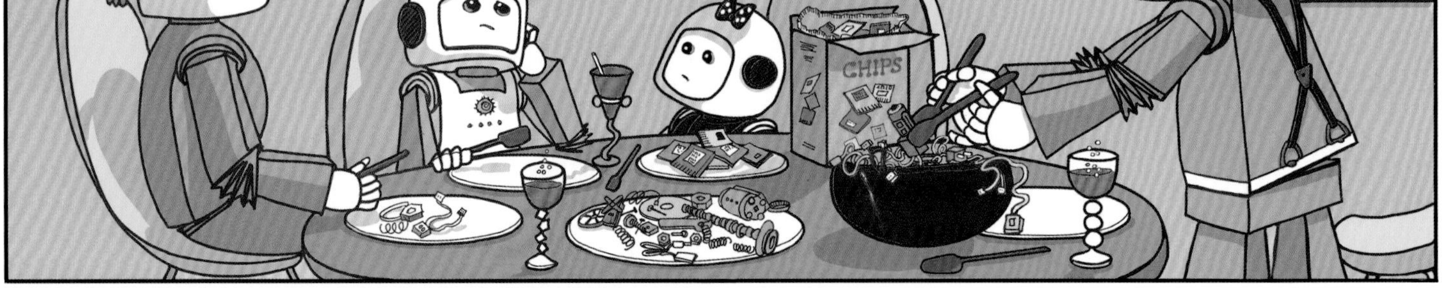
What's wrong, Roby? Didn't you save the day today?
I save the day every day. It's boring! Why can't I be a superhero in the real world?
CHIPS

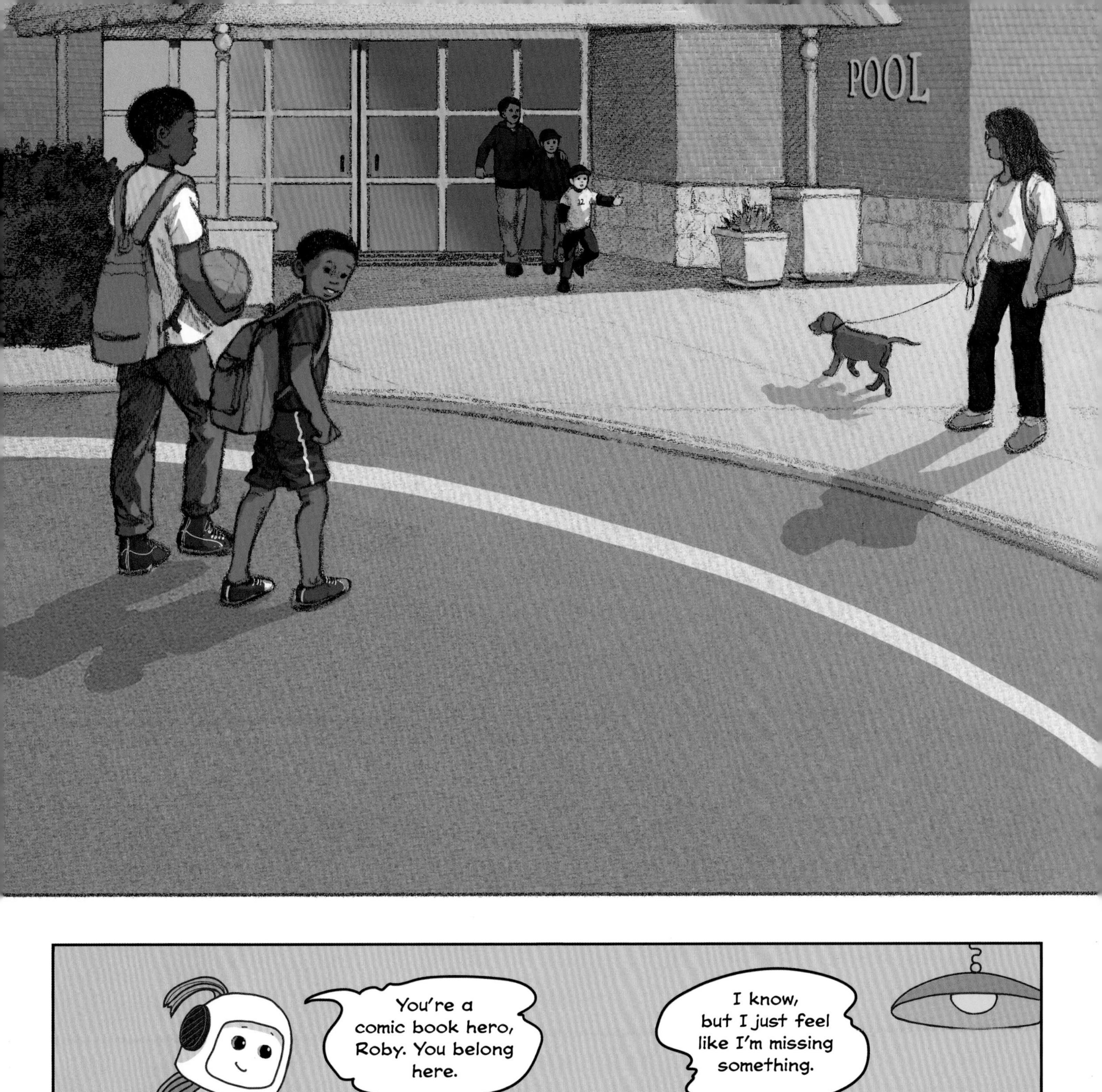
POOL

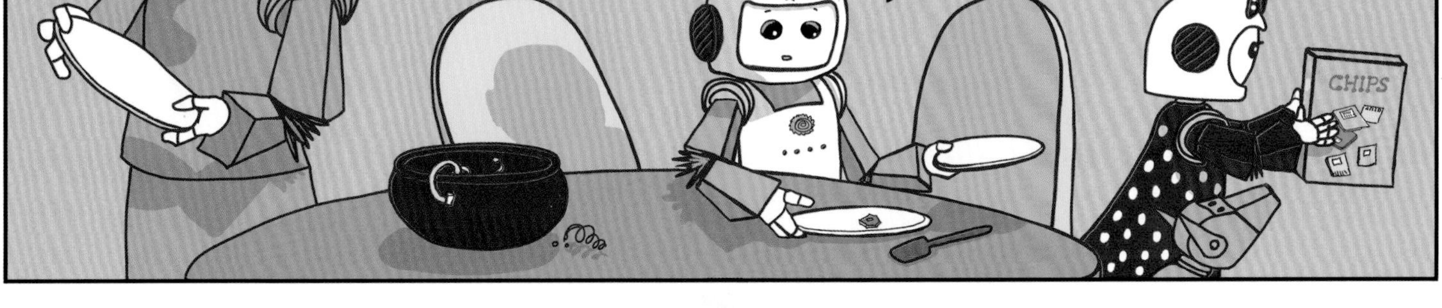
You're a comic book hero, Roby. You belong here.
I know, but I just feel like I'm missing something.
CHIPS

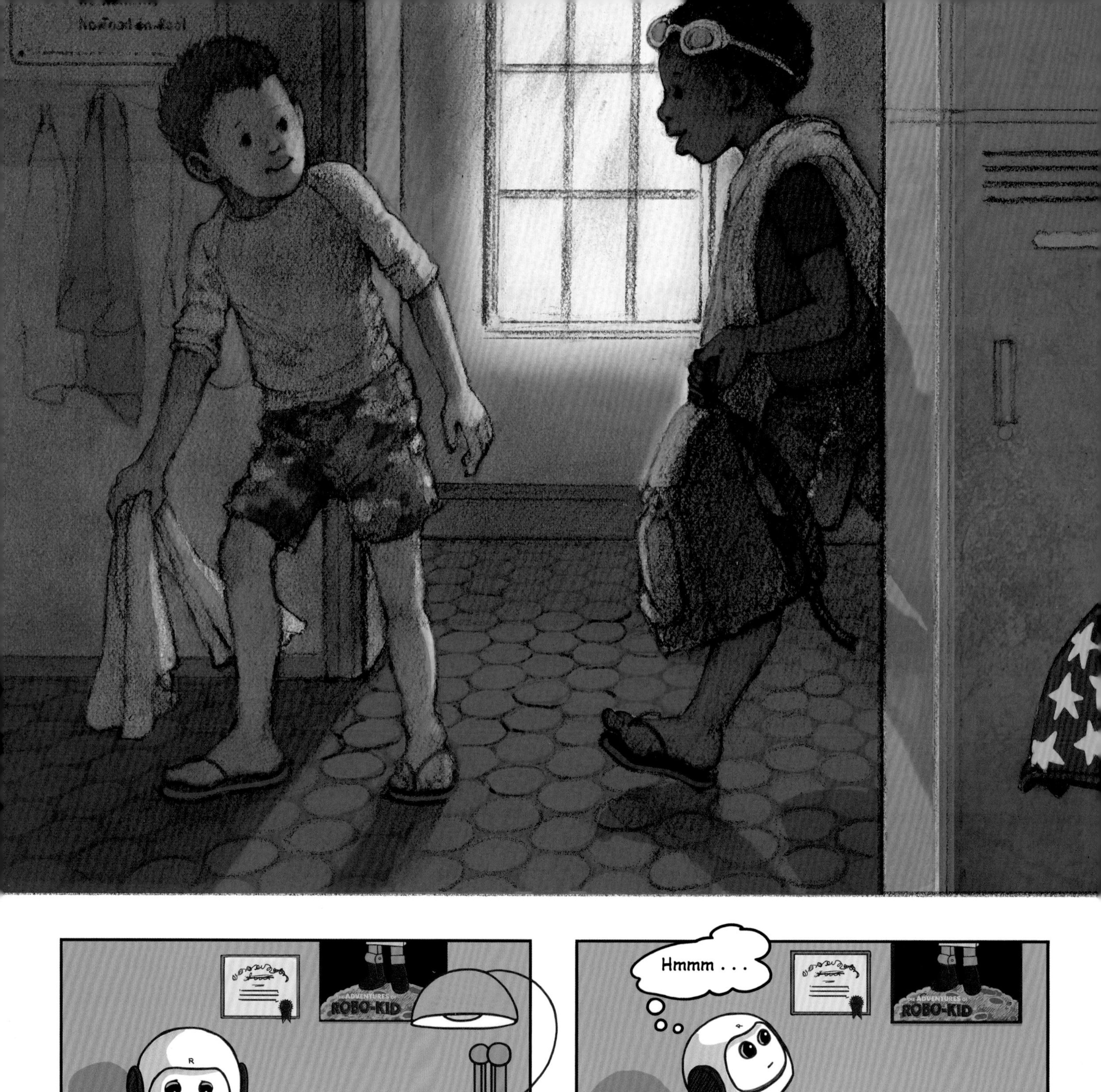

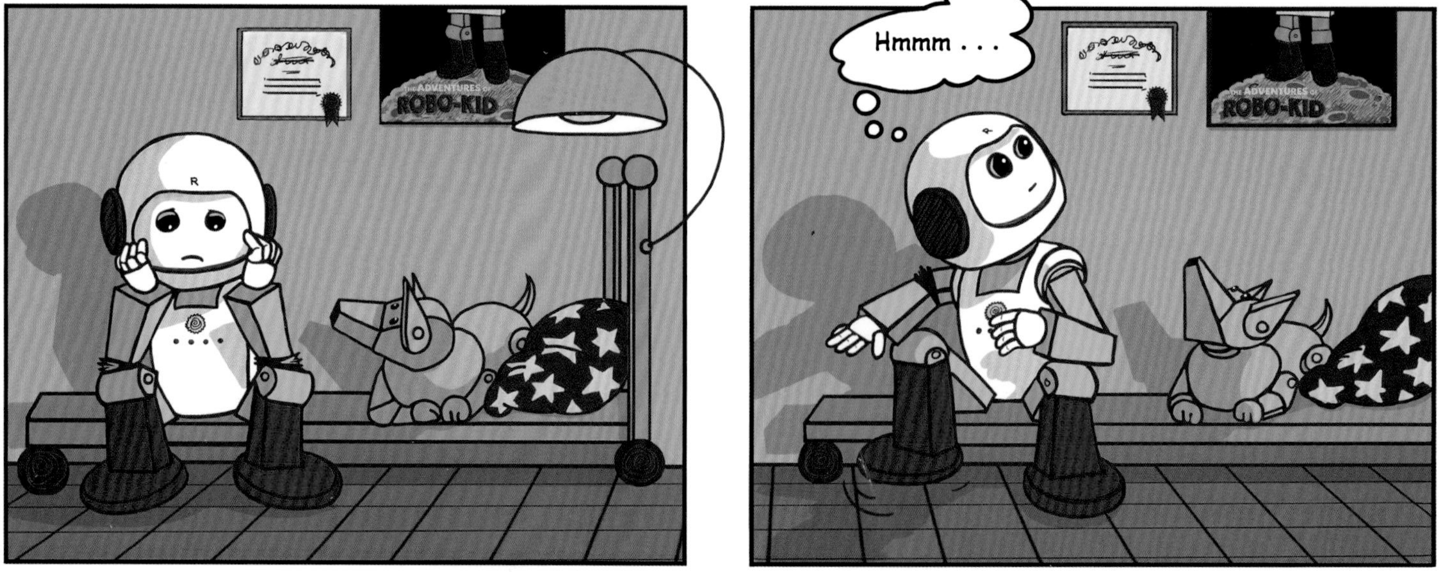
THE ADVENTURES OF ROBO-KID
Hmmm . . .
THE ADVENTURES OF ROBO-KID

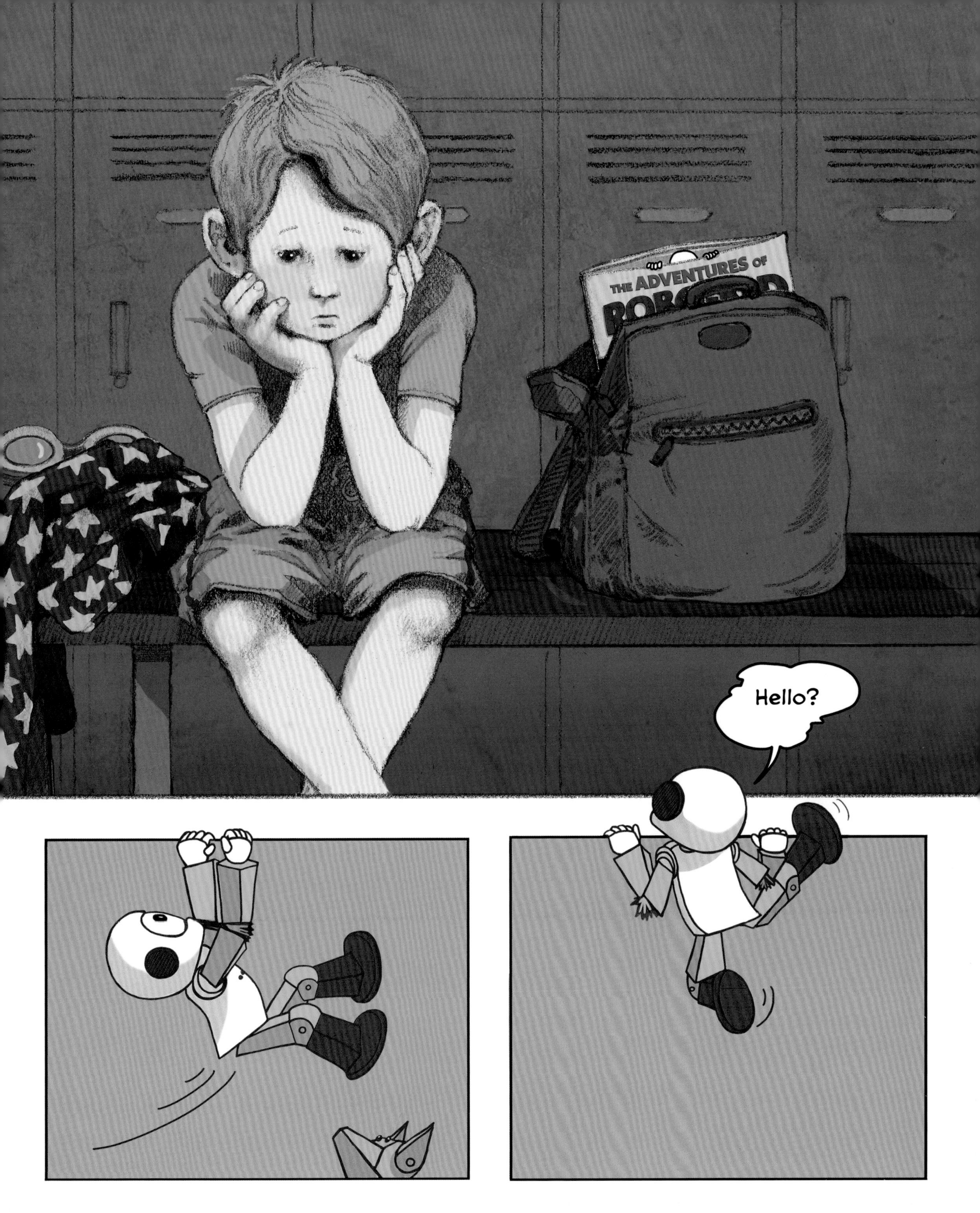
THE ADVENTURES OF
Hello?

"Huh?
Robo-Kid?"

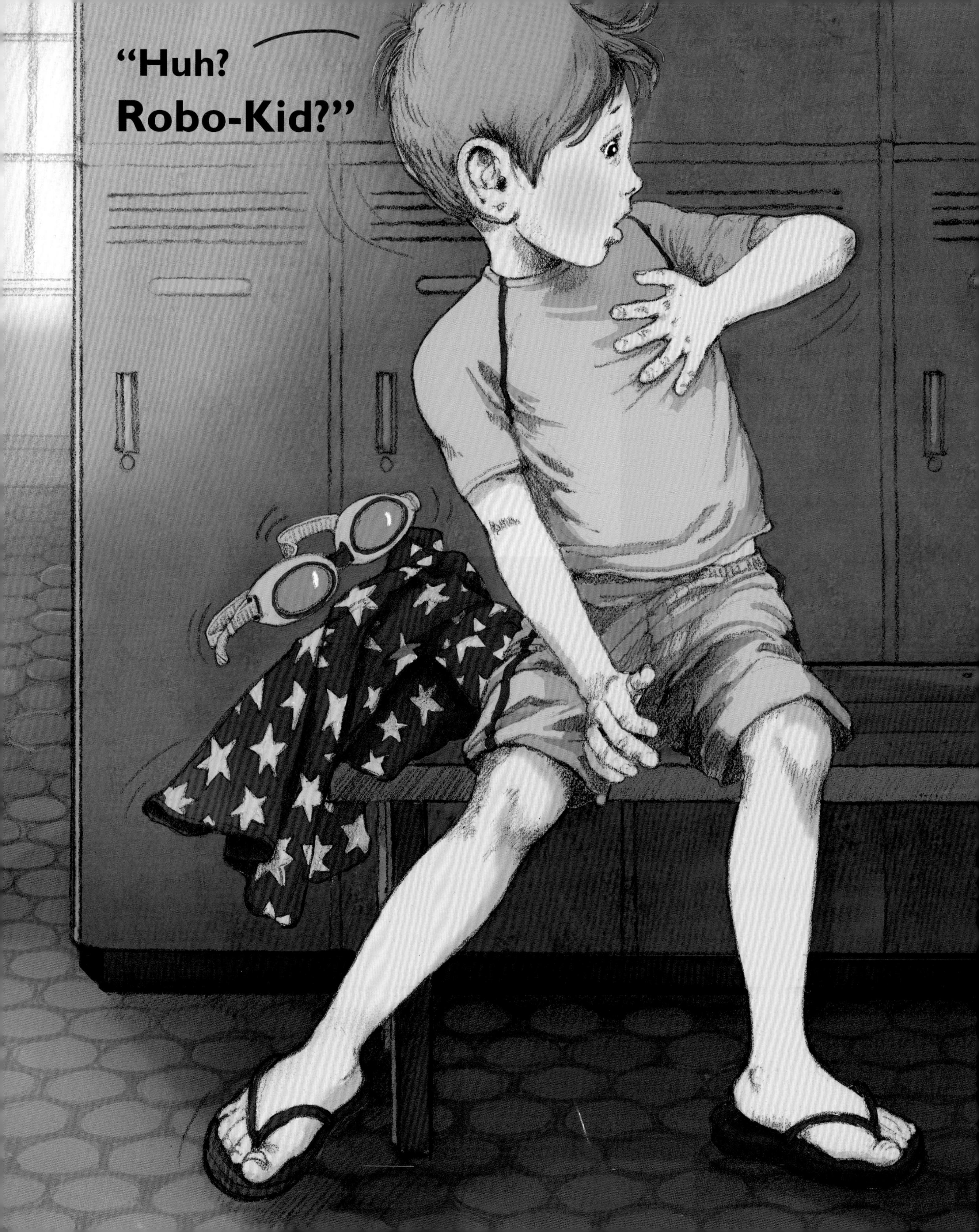

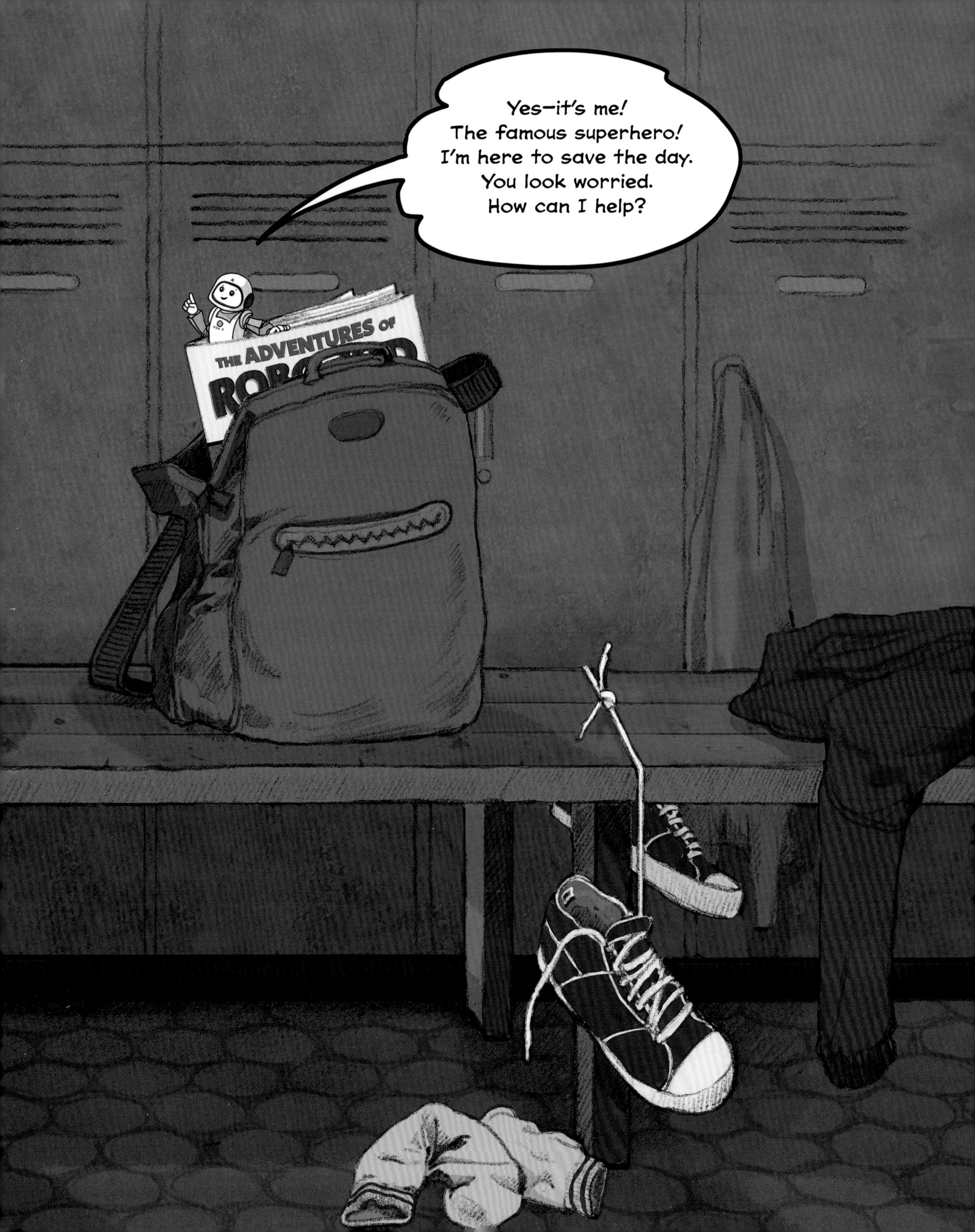
Yes—it's me!
The famous superhero!
I'm here to save the day.
You look worried.
How can I help?
THE ADVENTURES OF

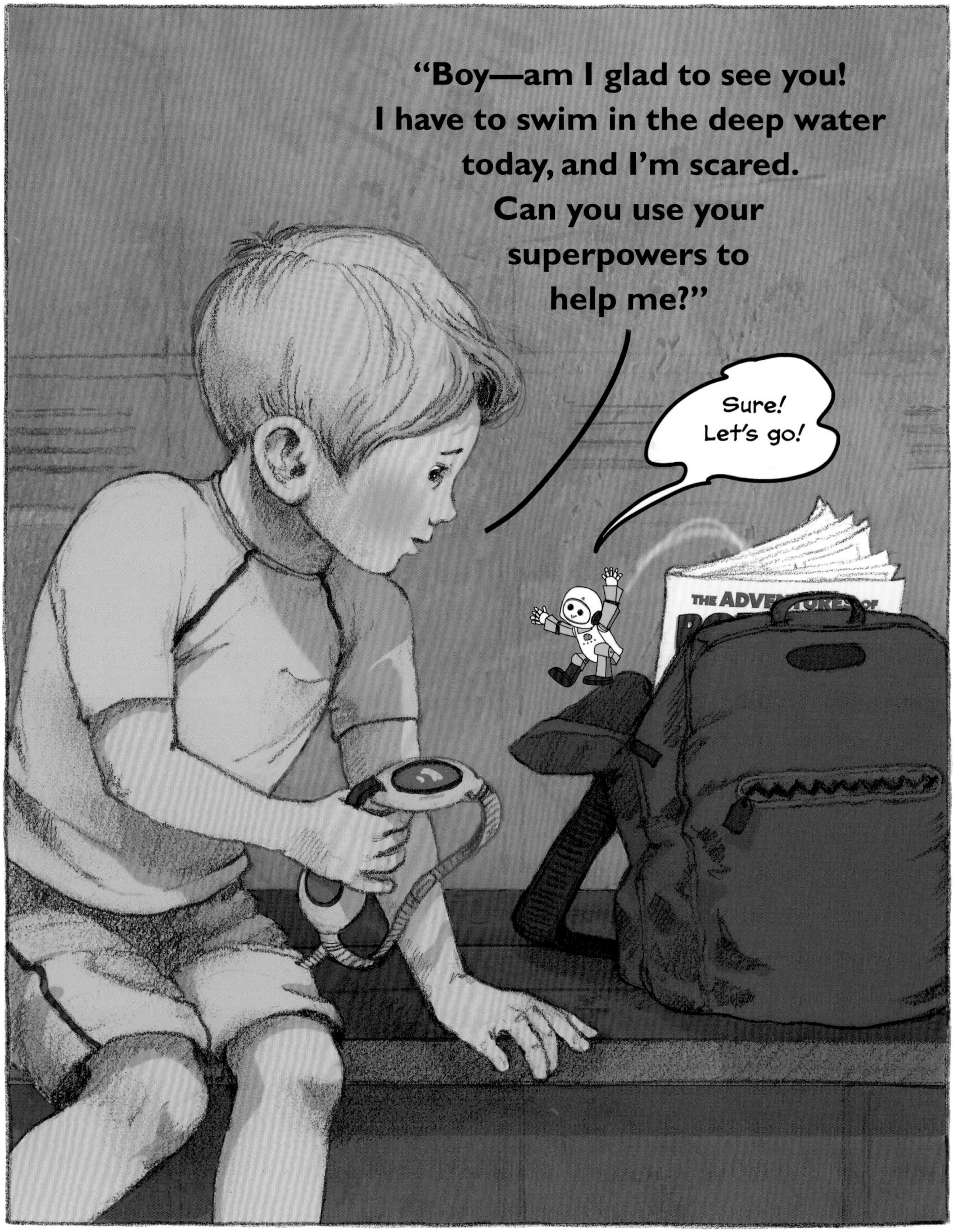
"Boy—am I glad to see you! I have to swim in the deep water today, and I'm scared. Can you use your superpowers to help me?"
Sure! Let's go!

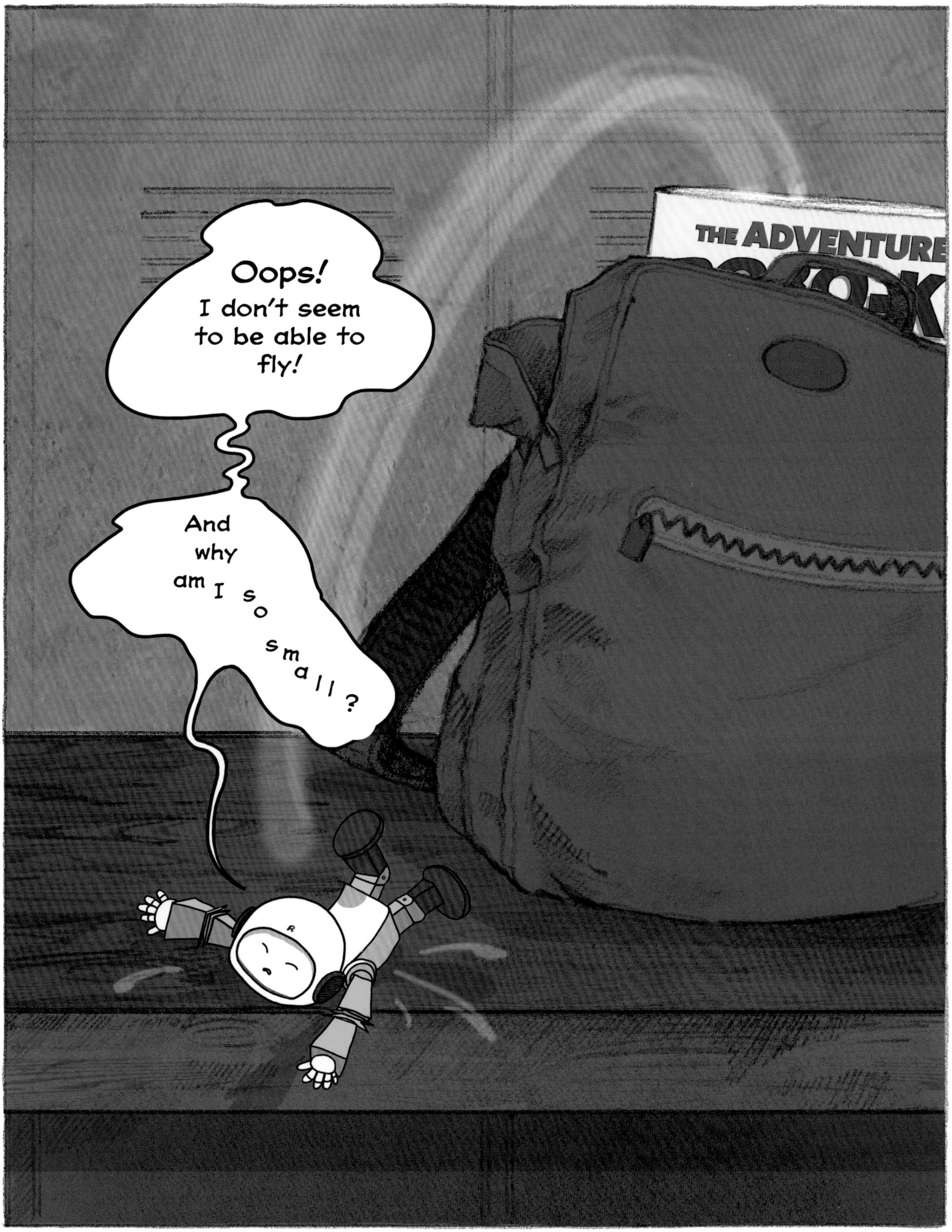
THE ADVENTURE
Oops! I don't seem to be able to fly!
And why am I so small?

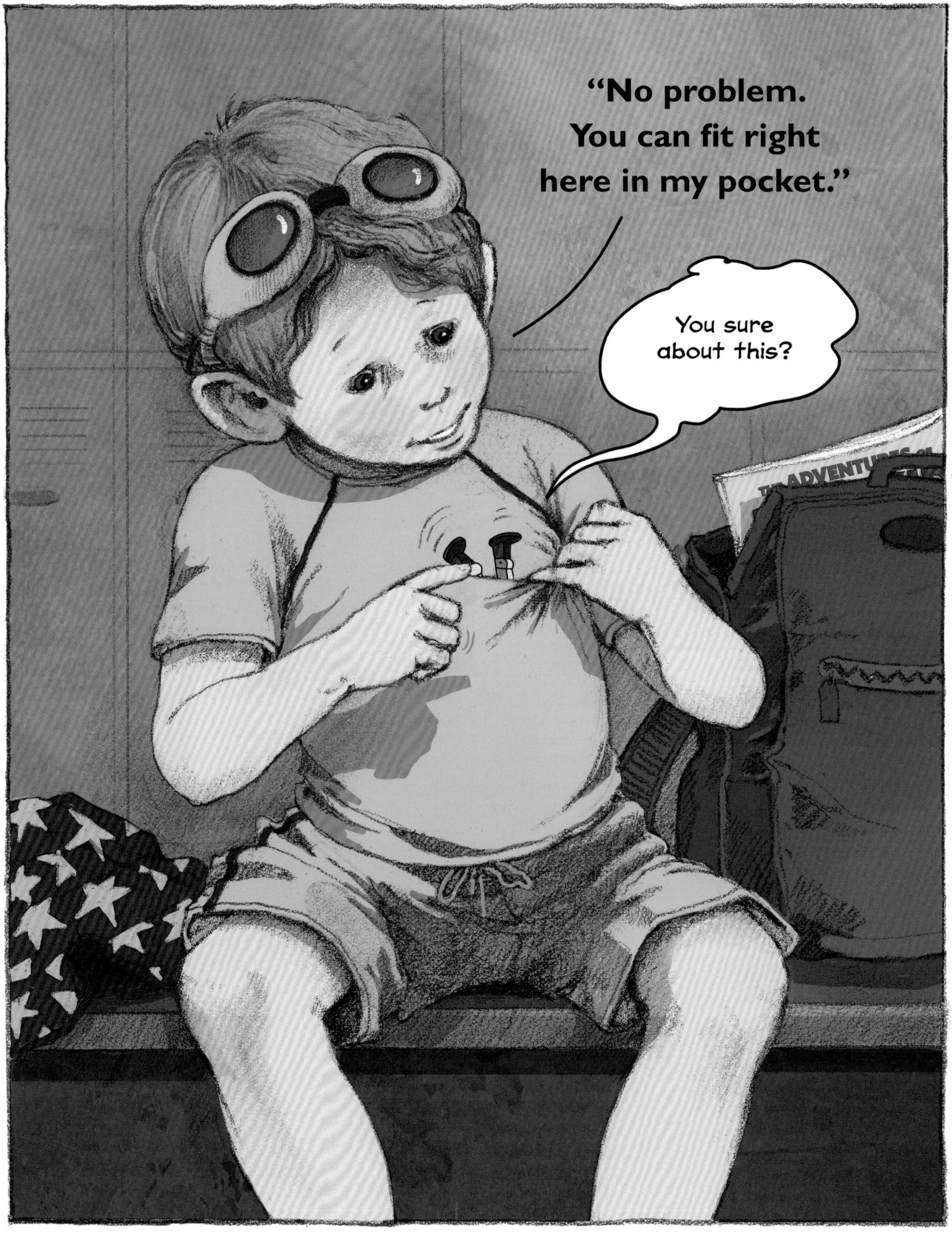
"No problem. You can fit right here in my pocket."
You sure about this?

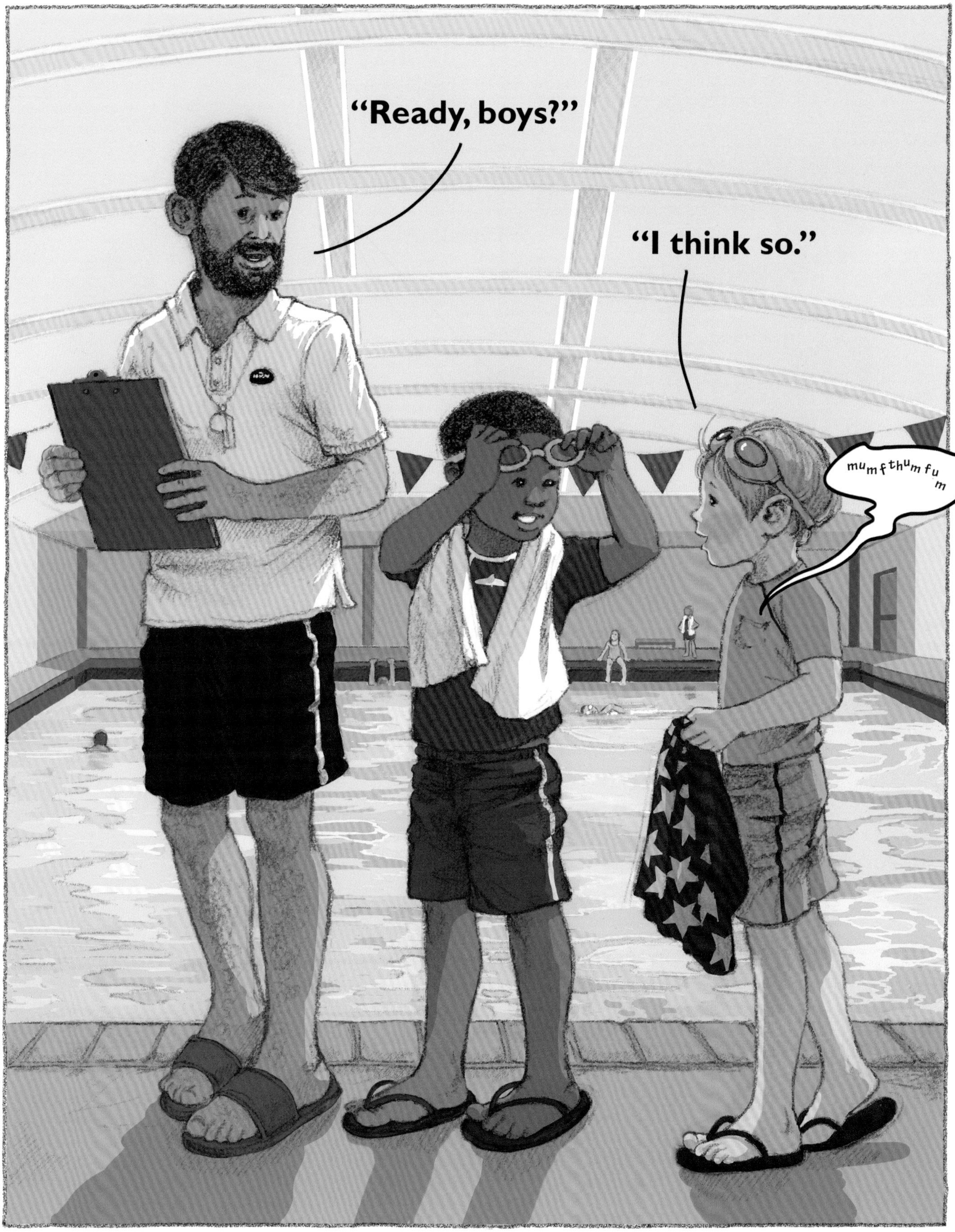
"Ready, boys?"
"I think so."
mumfthumfum

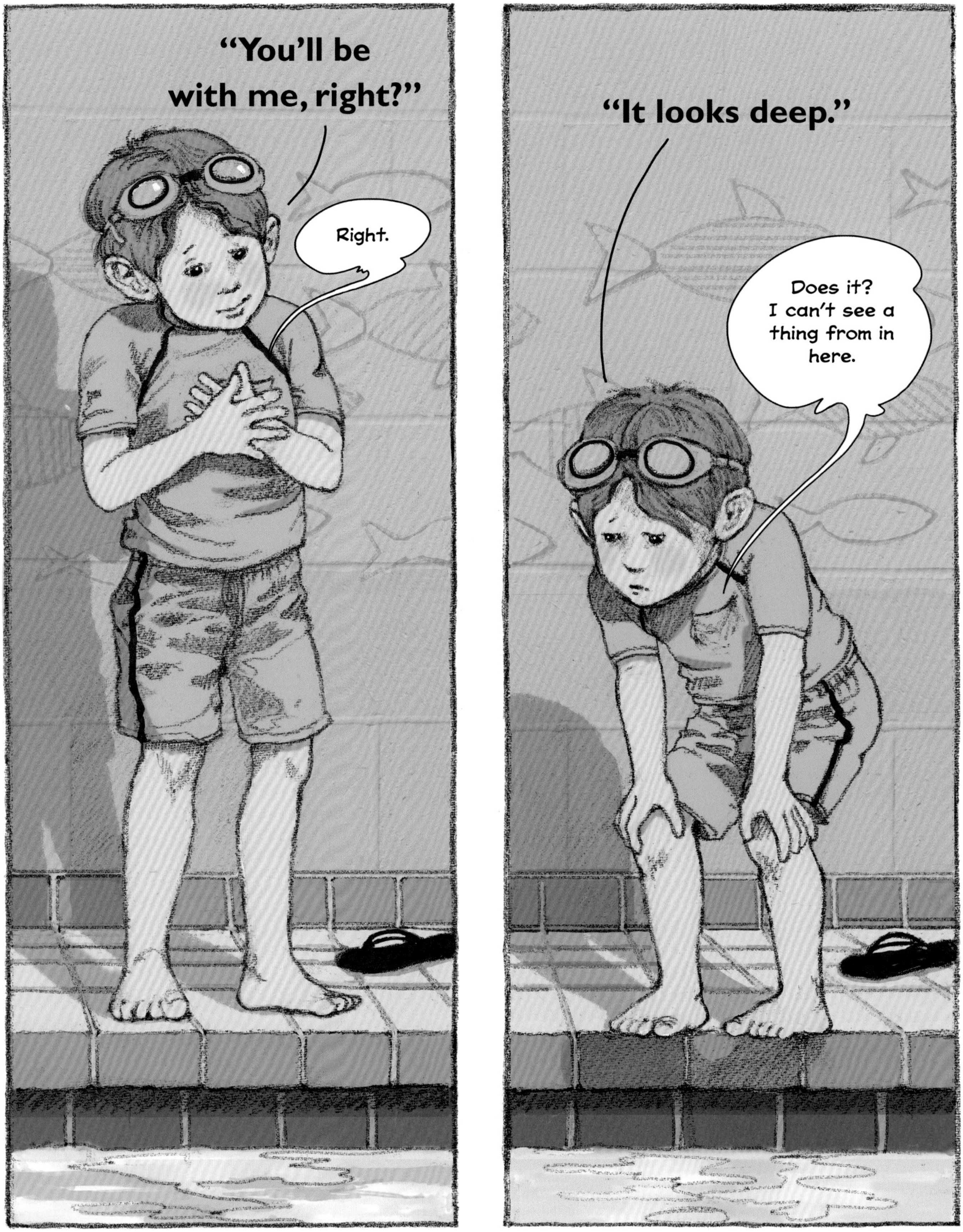
"You'll be with me, right?"
Right.
"It looks deep."
Does it? I can't see a thing from in here.

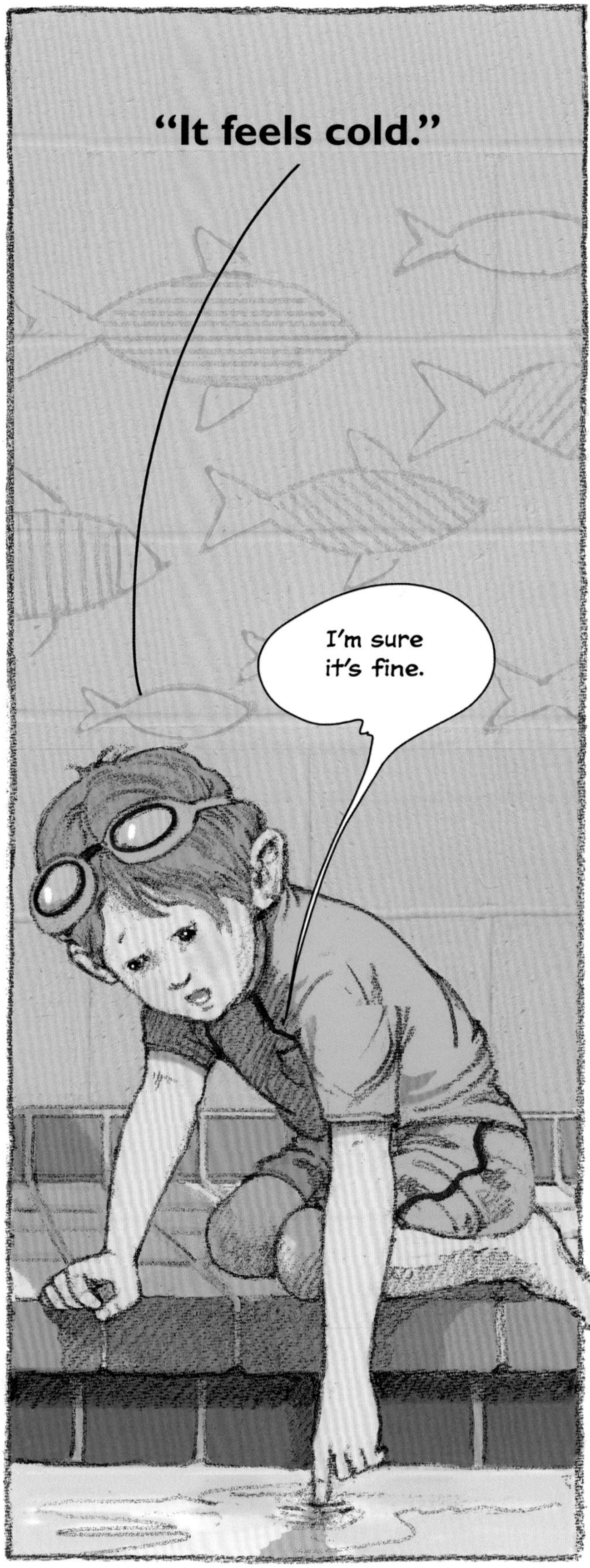
"It feels cold."
I'm sure it's fine.

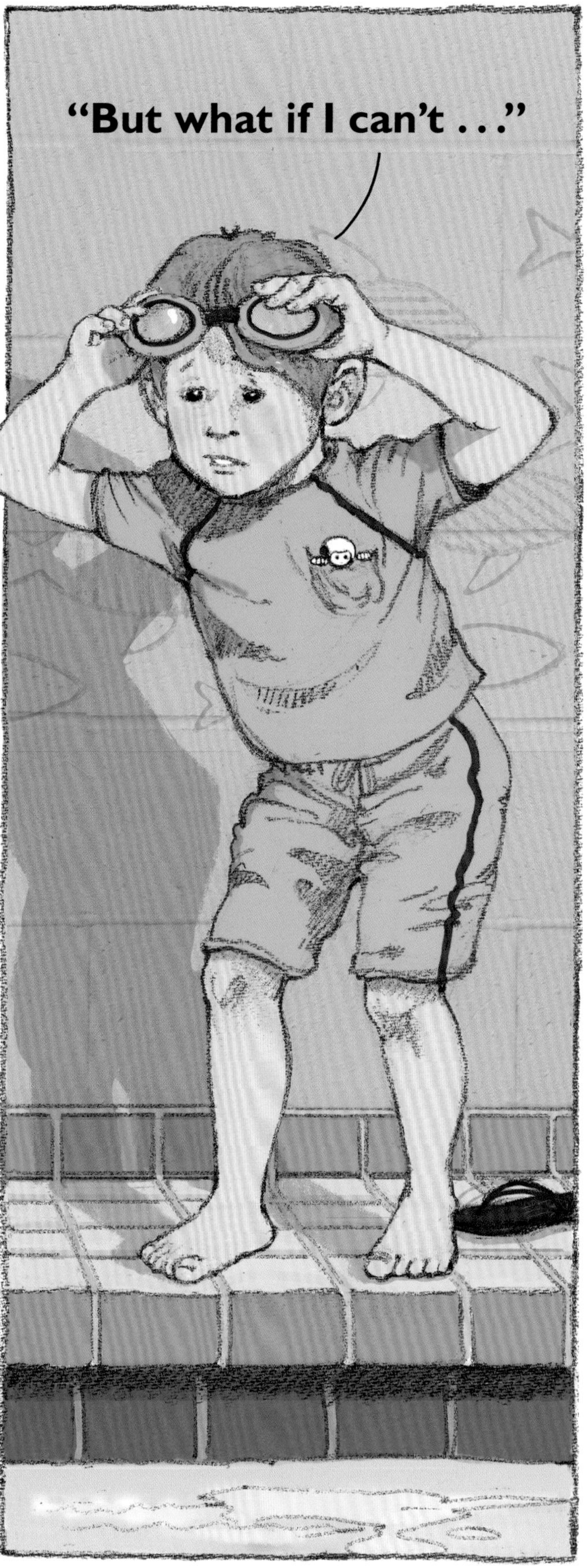
"But what if I can't . . ."

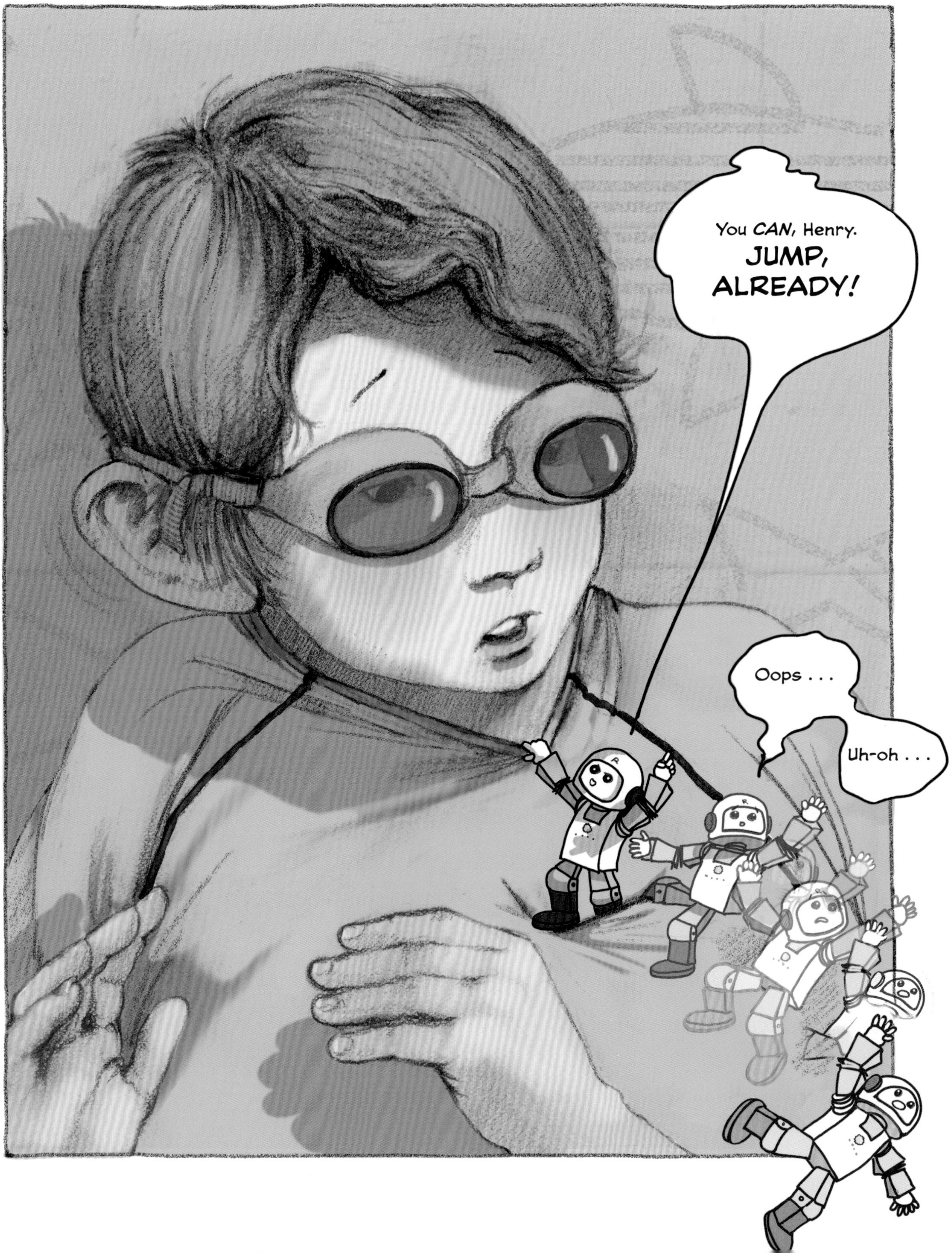
You CAN, Henry.
JUMP, ALREADY!
Oops . . .
Uh-oh . . .

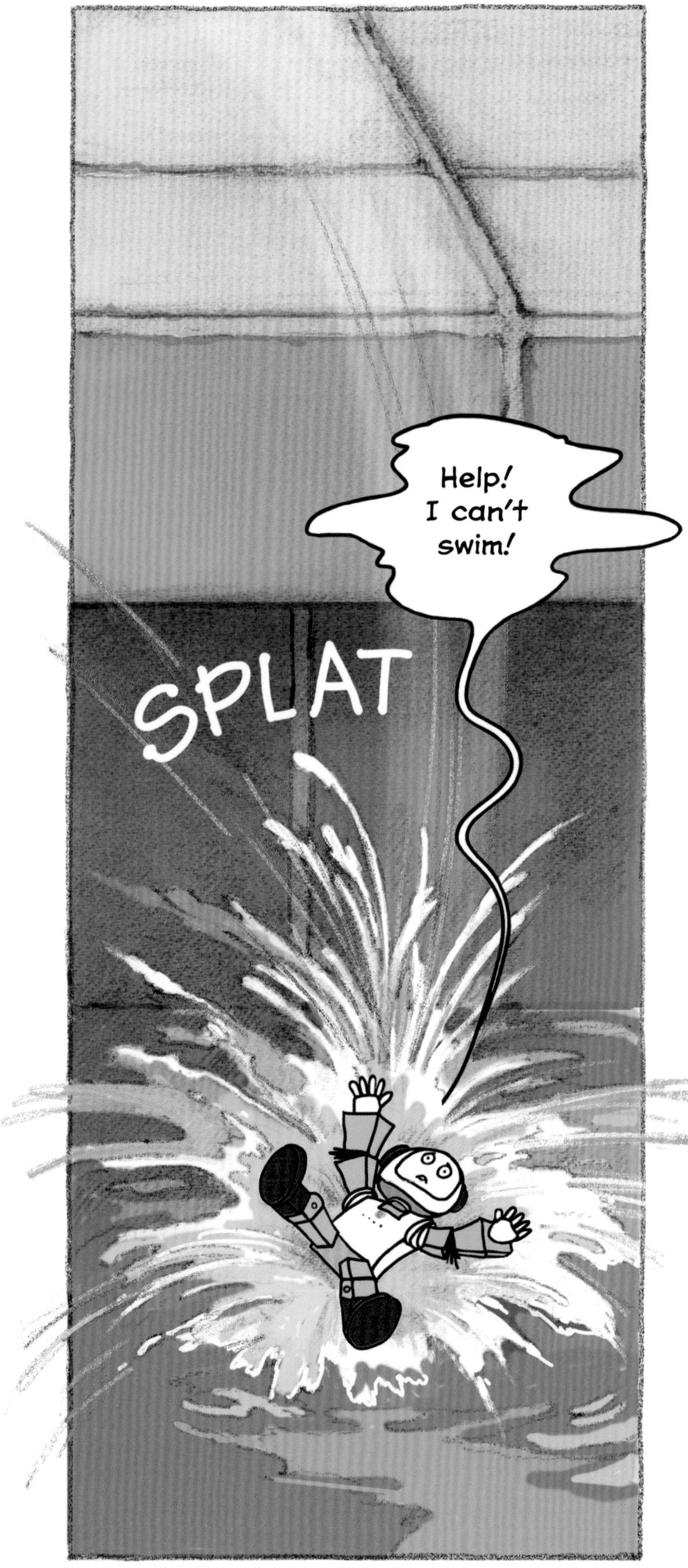
Help! I can't swim!
SPLAT

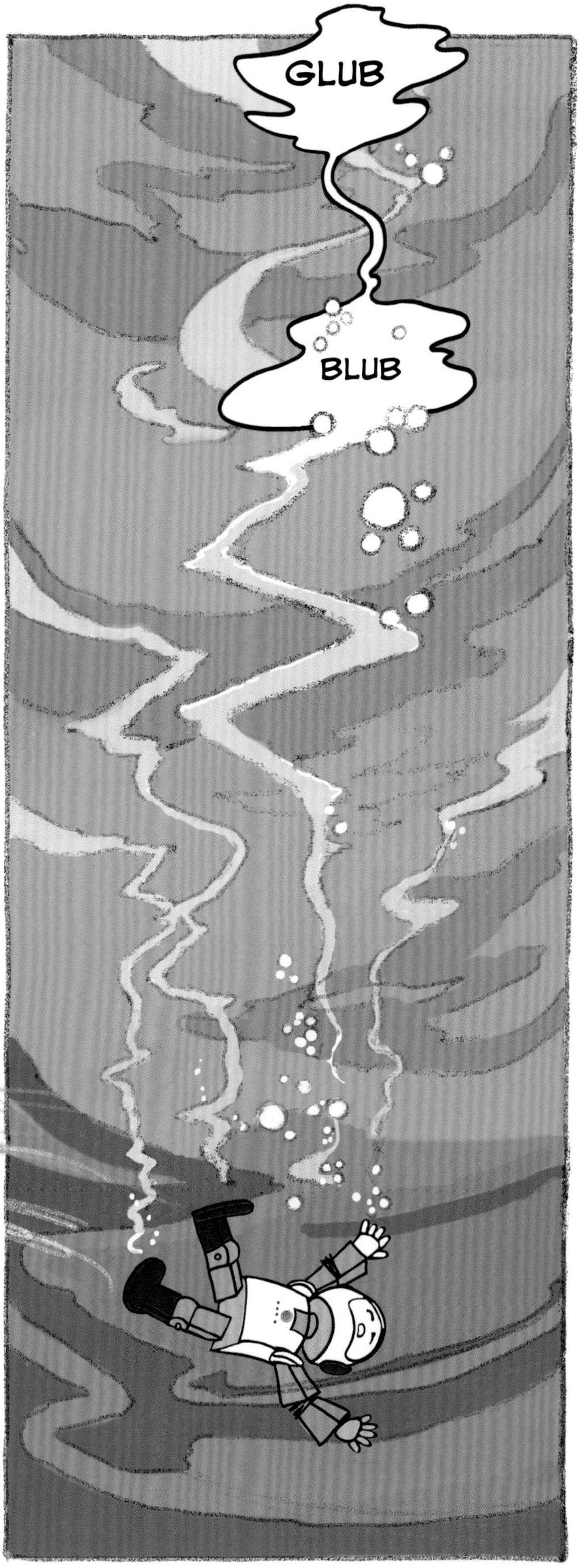
GLUB
BLUB

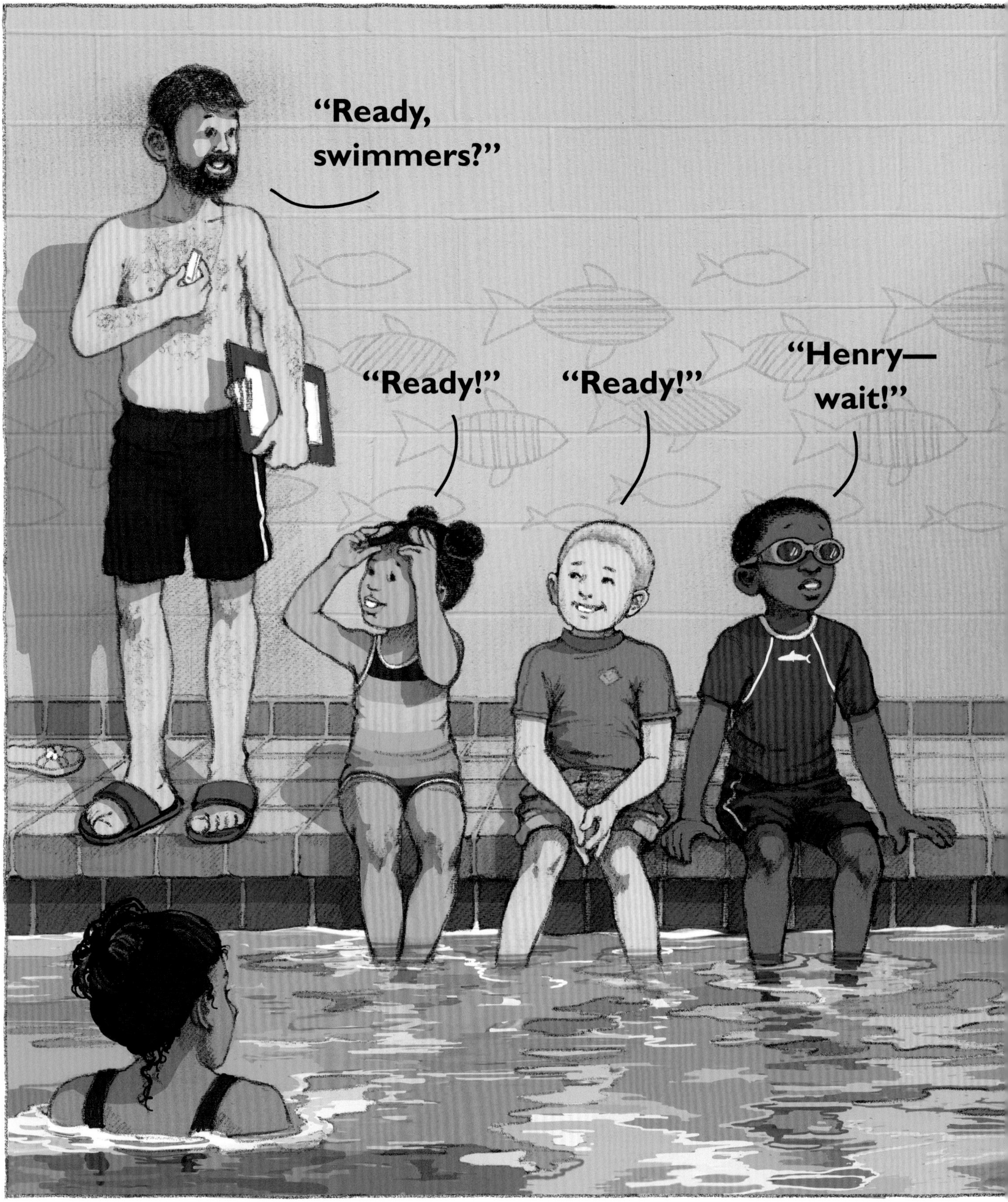
"Ready,
swimmers?"
"Ready!"
"Ready!"
"Henry—
wait!"

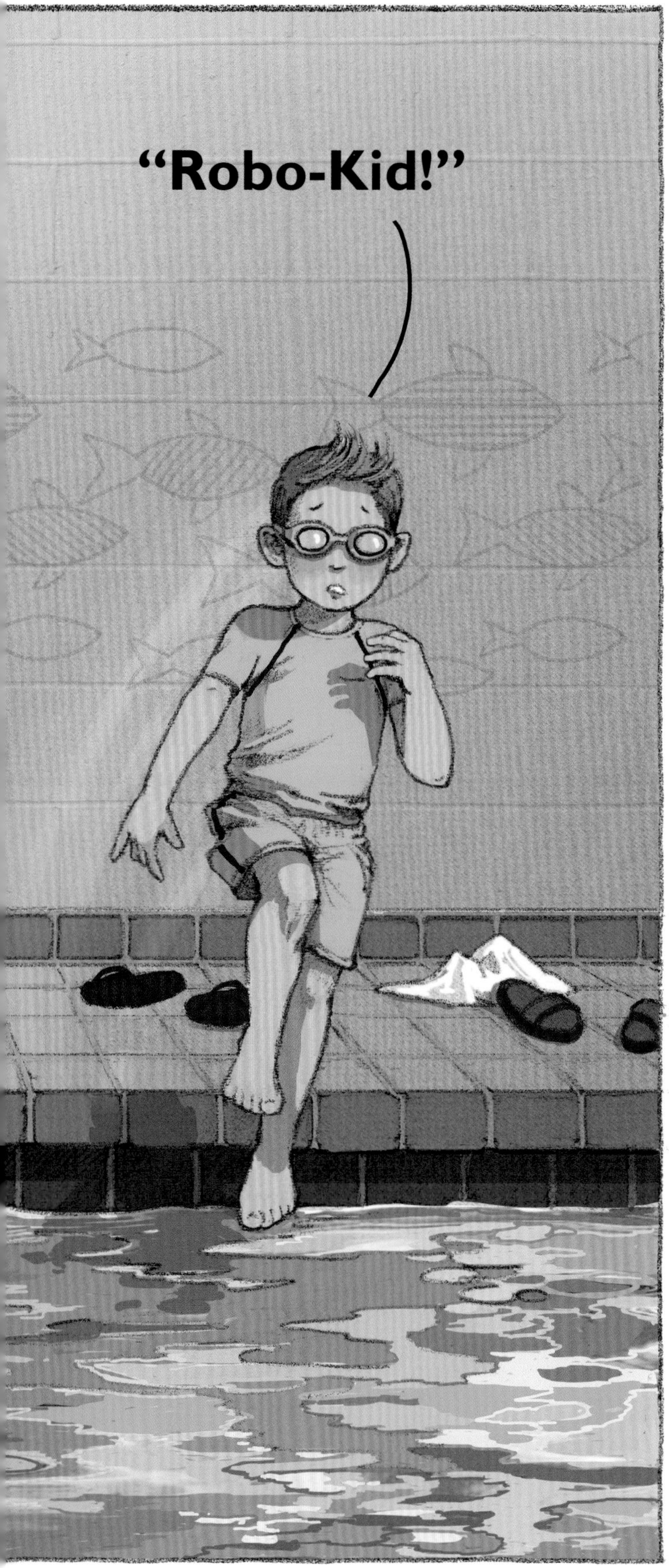
"Robo-Kid!"

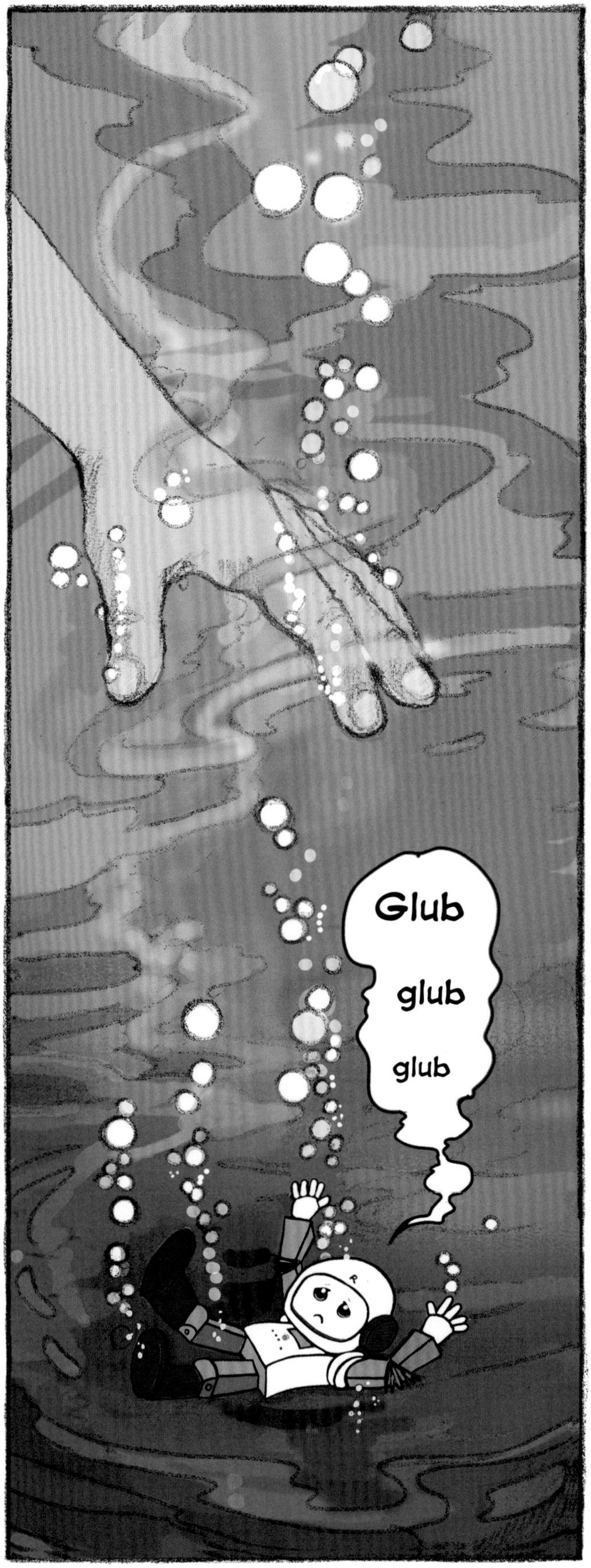
Glub
glub
glub

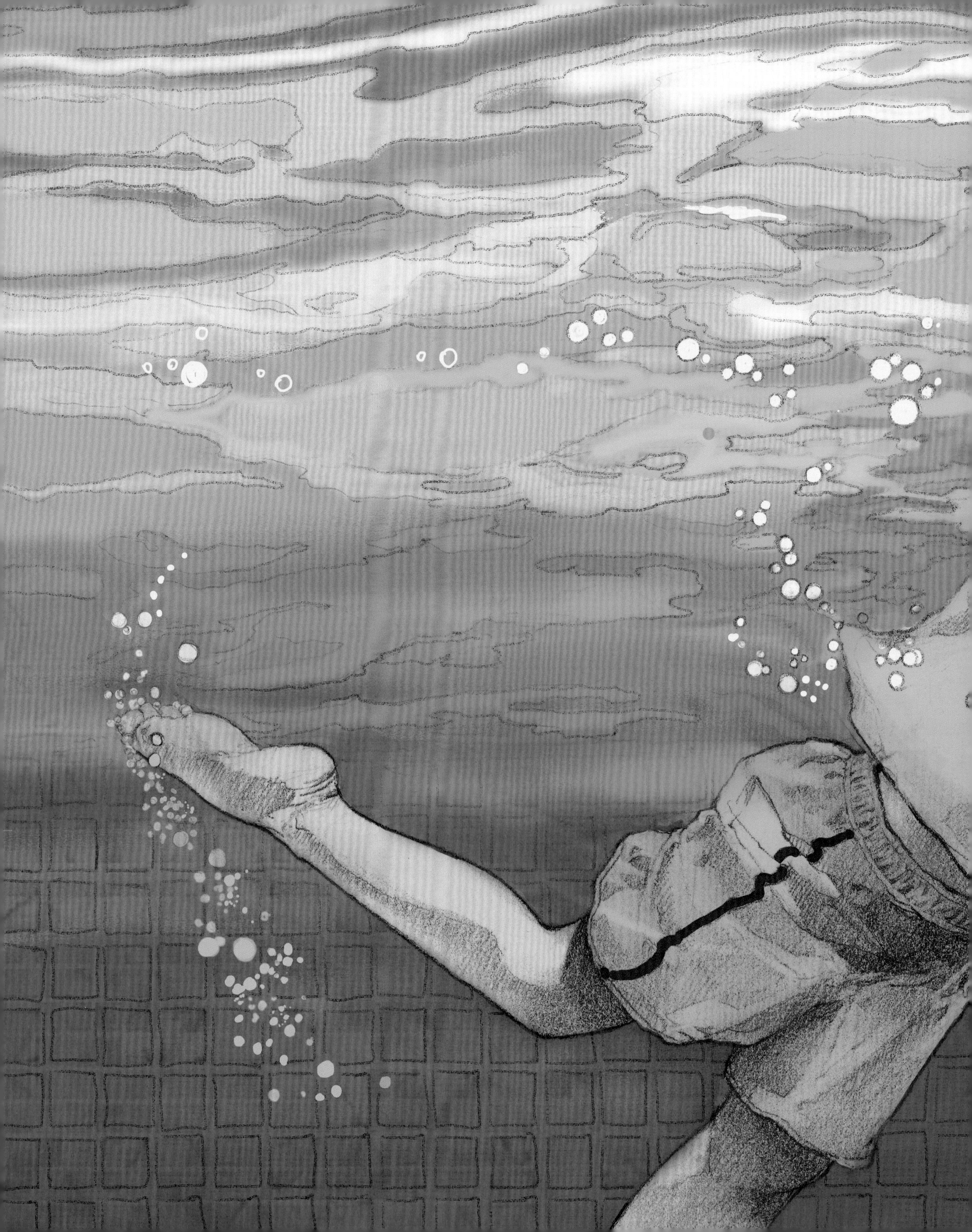

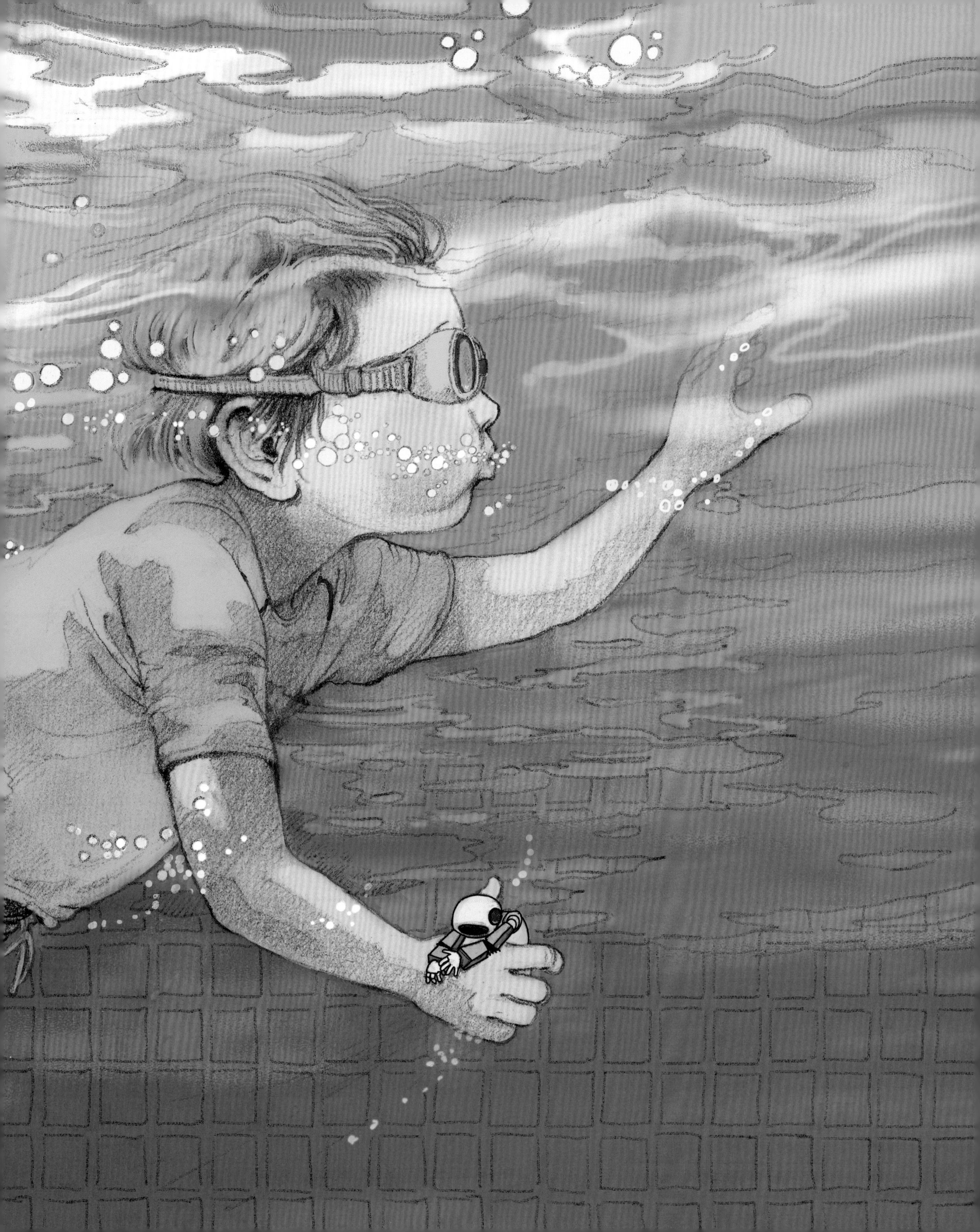

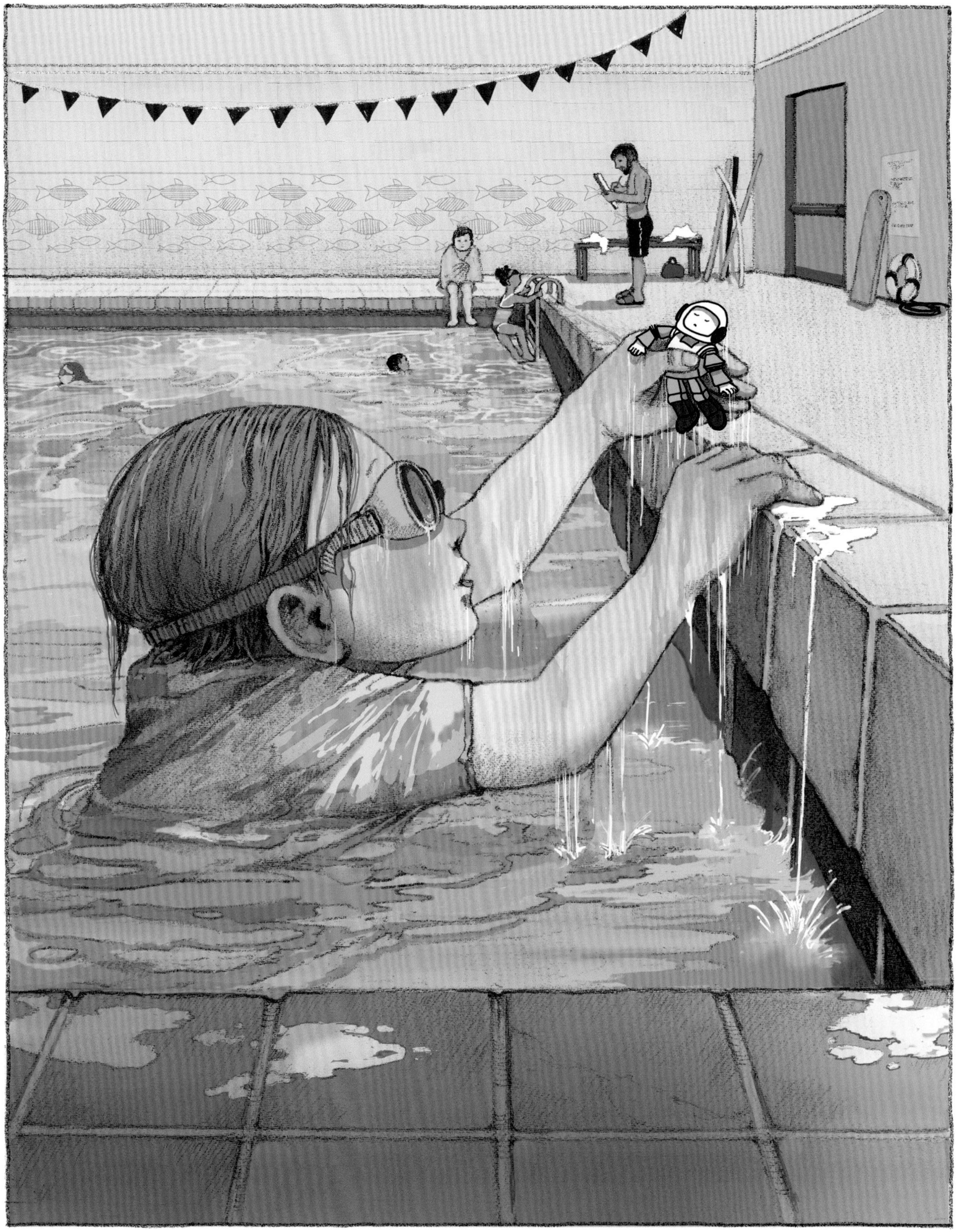

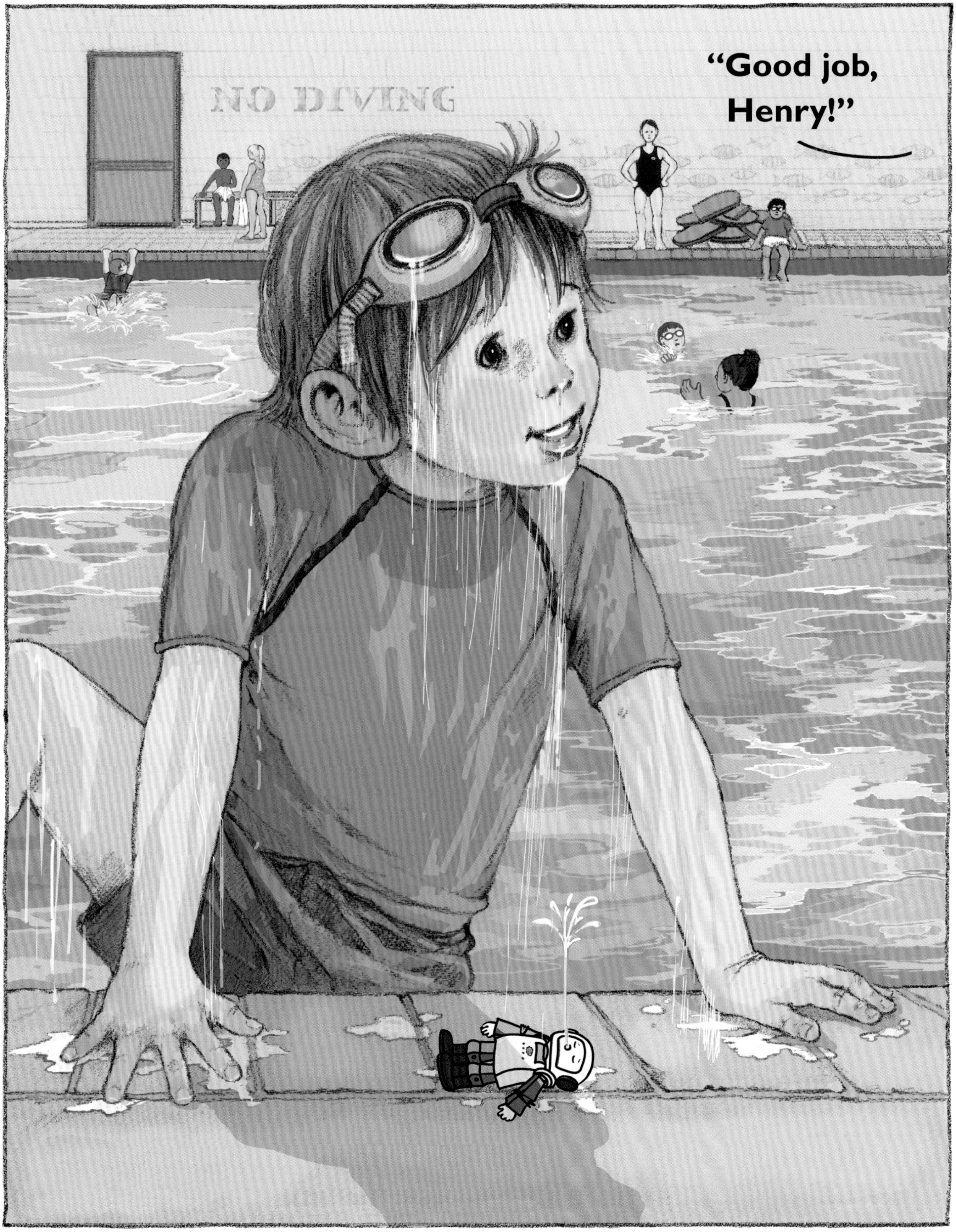
NO DIVING
"Good job, Henry!"

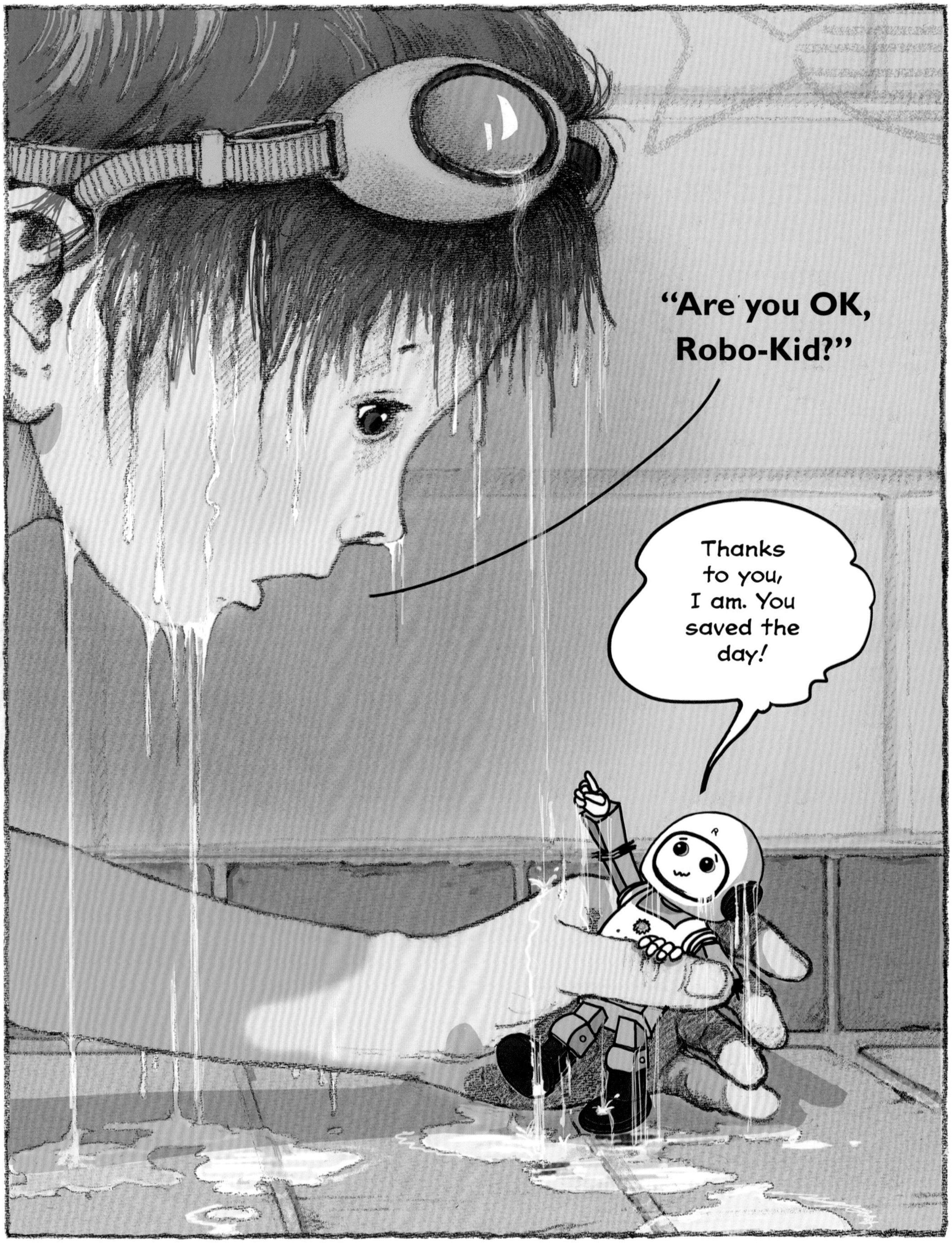
"Are you OK, Robo-Kid?"
Thanks to you, I am. You saved the day!

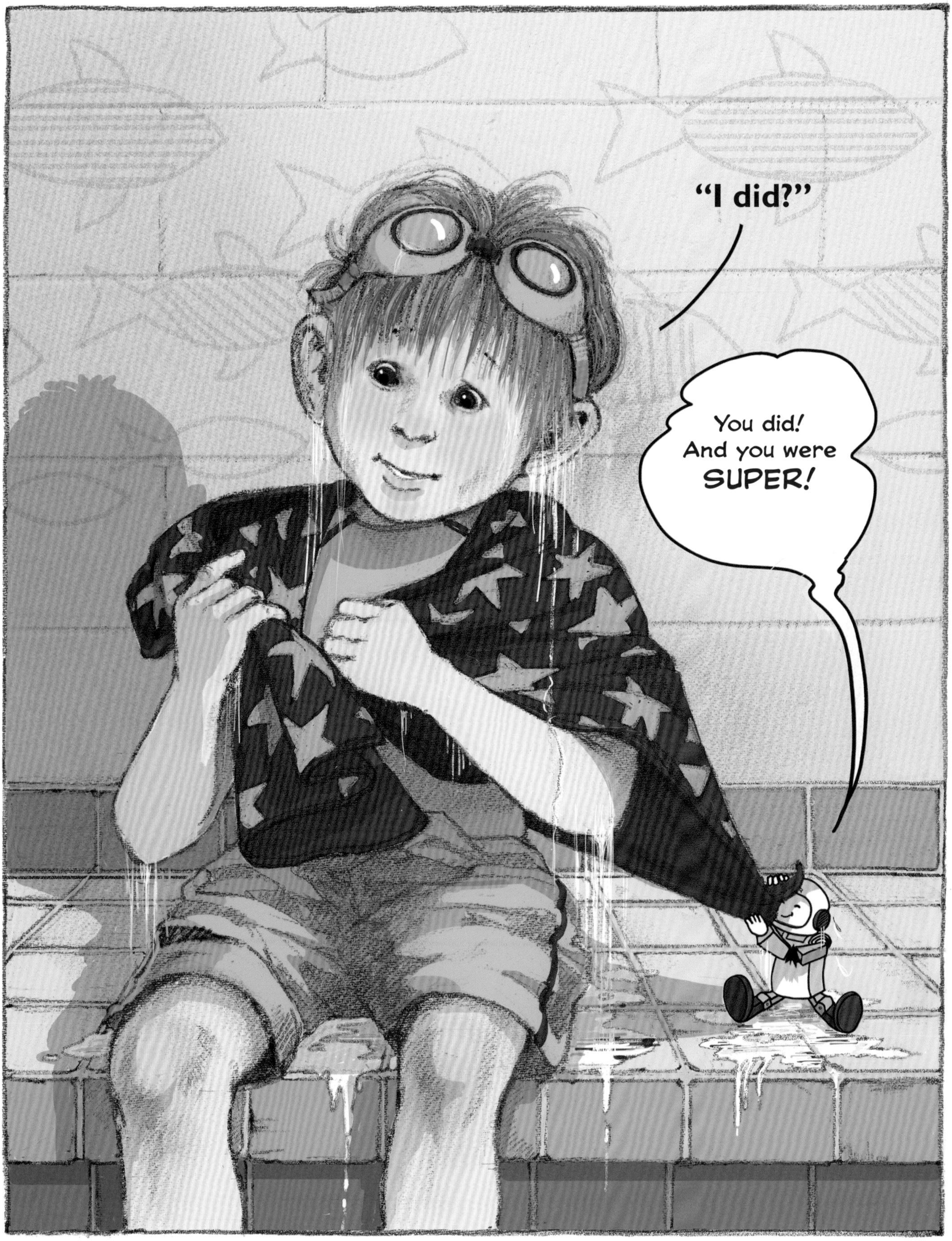
"I did?"
You did! And you were SUPER!

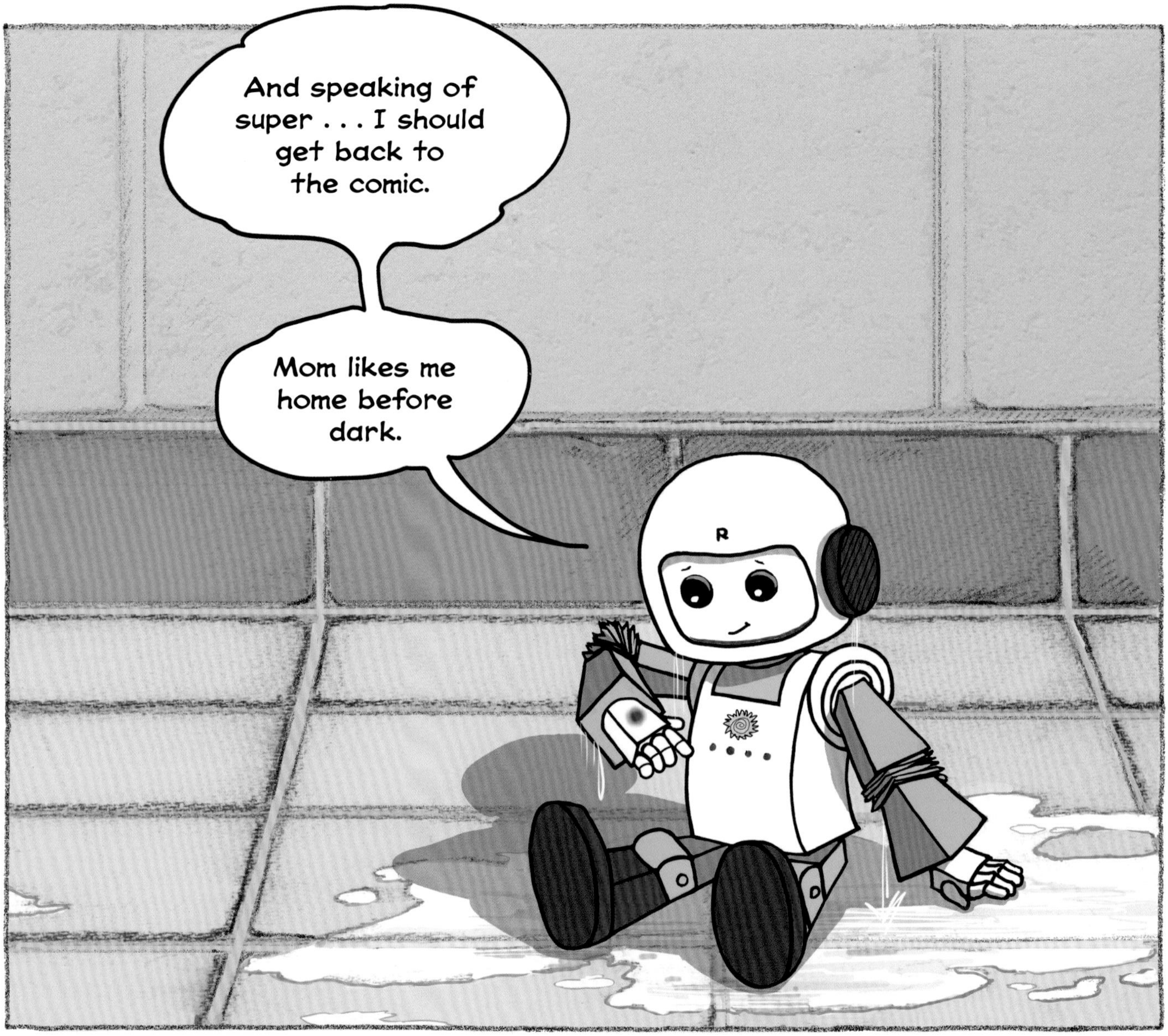
And speaking of super . . . I should get back to the comic.
Mom likes me home before dark.

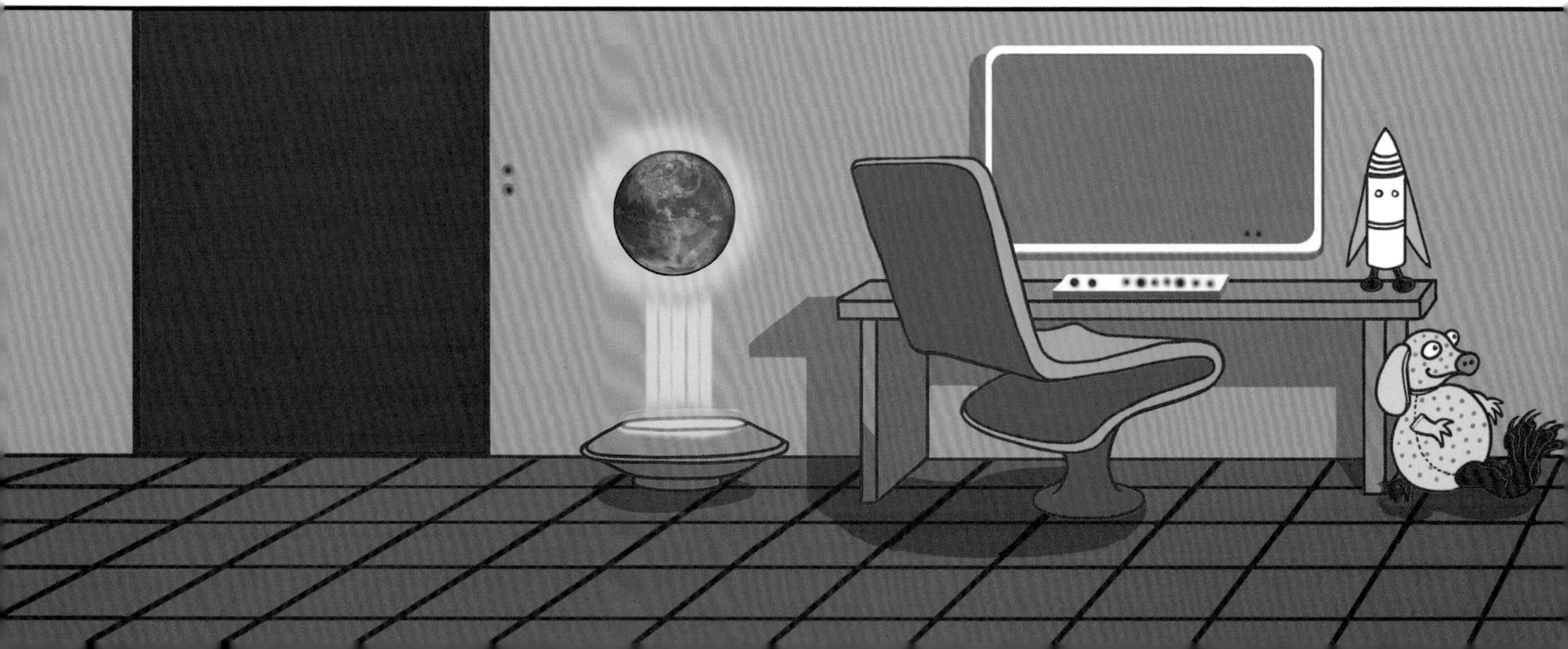

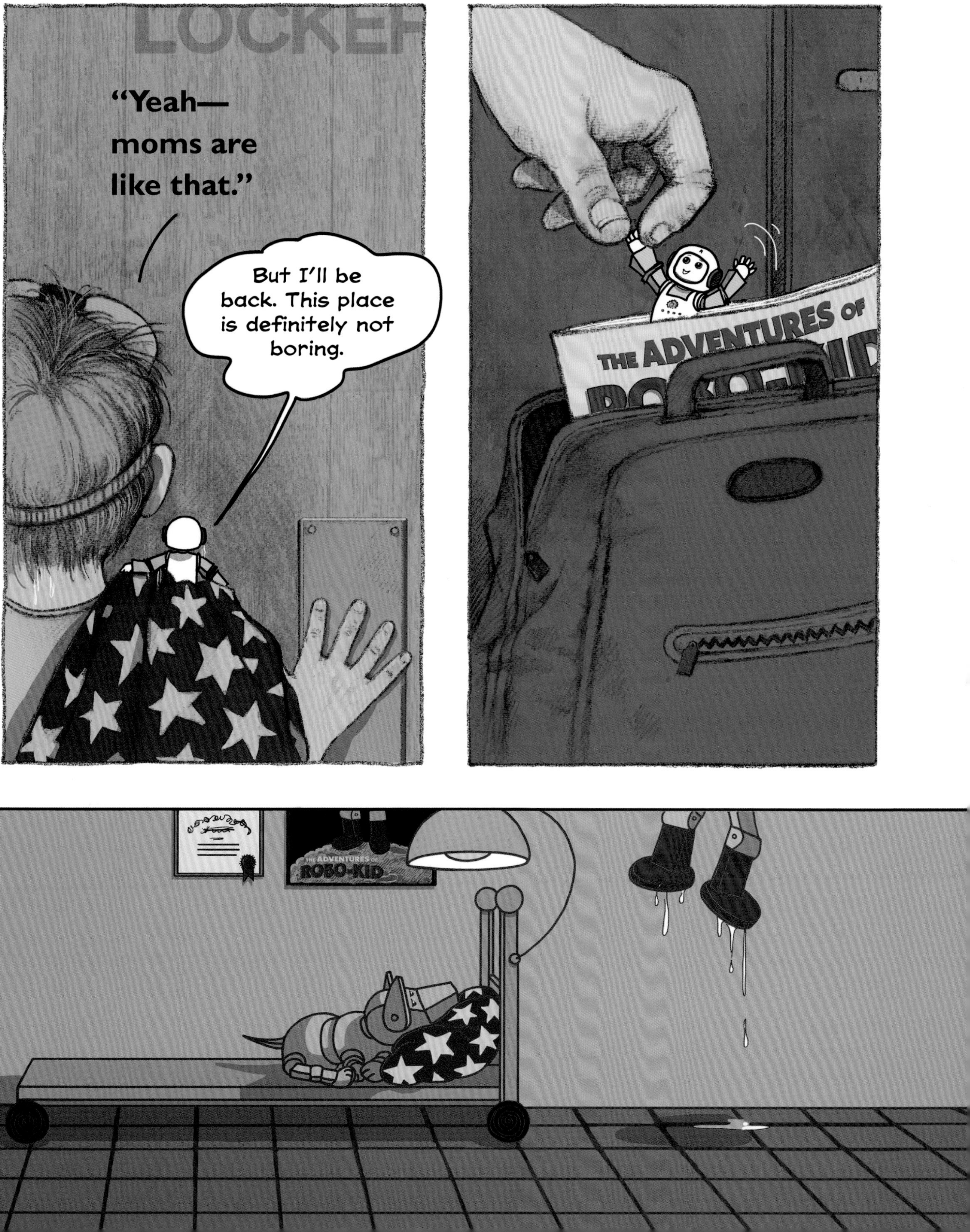
"Yeah—
moms are
like that."
But I'll be back. This place is definitely not boring.
THE ADVENTURES OF
THE ADVENTURES OF ROBO-KID

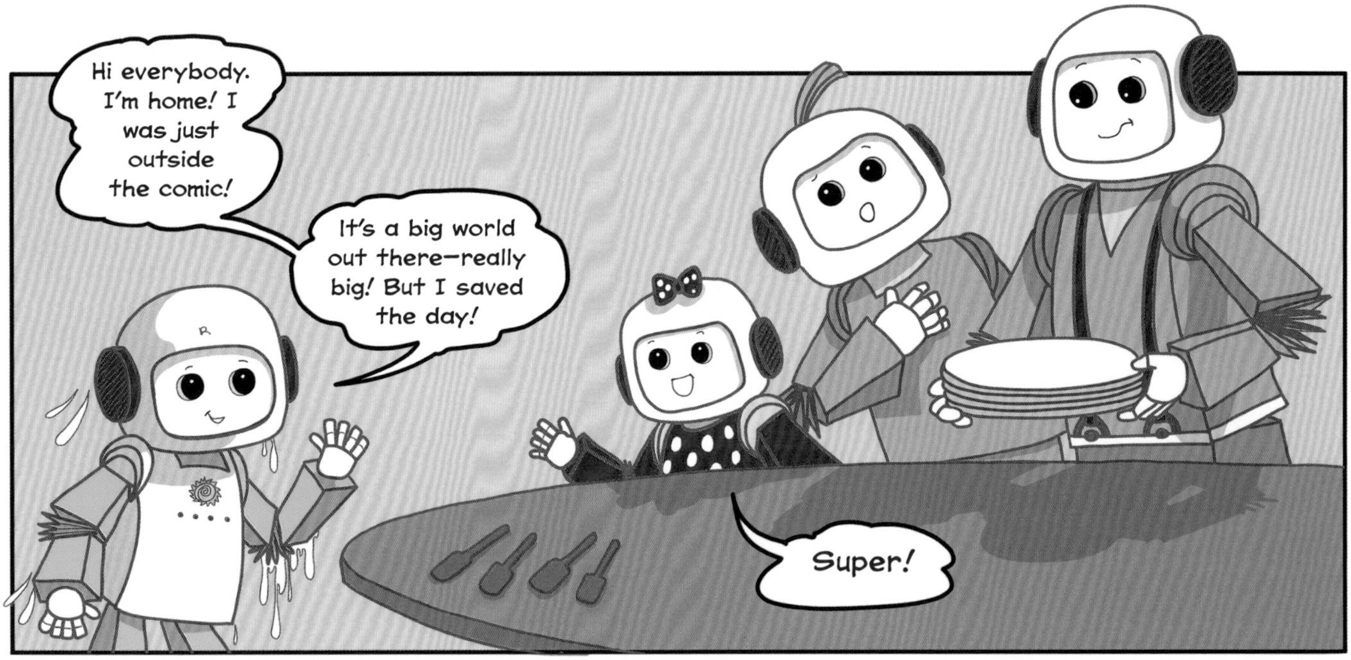
Hi everybody. I'm home! I was just outside the comic!
It's a big world out there—really big! But I saved the day!
Super!

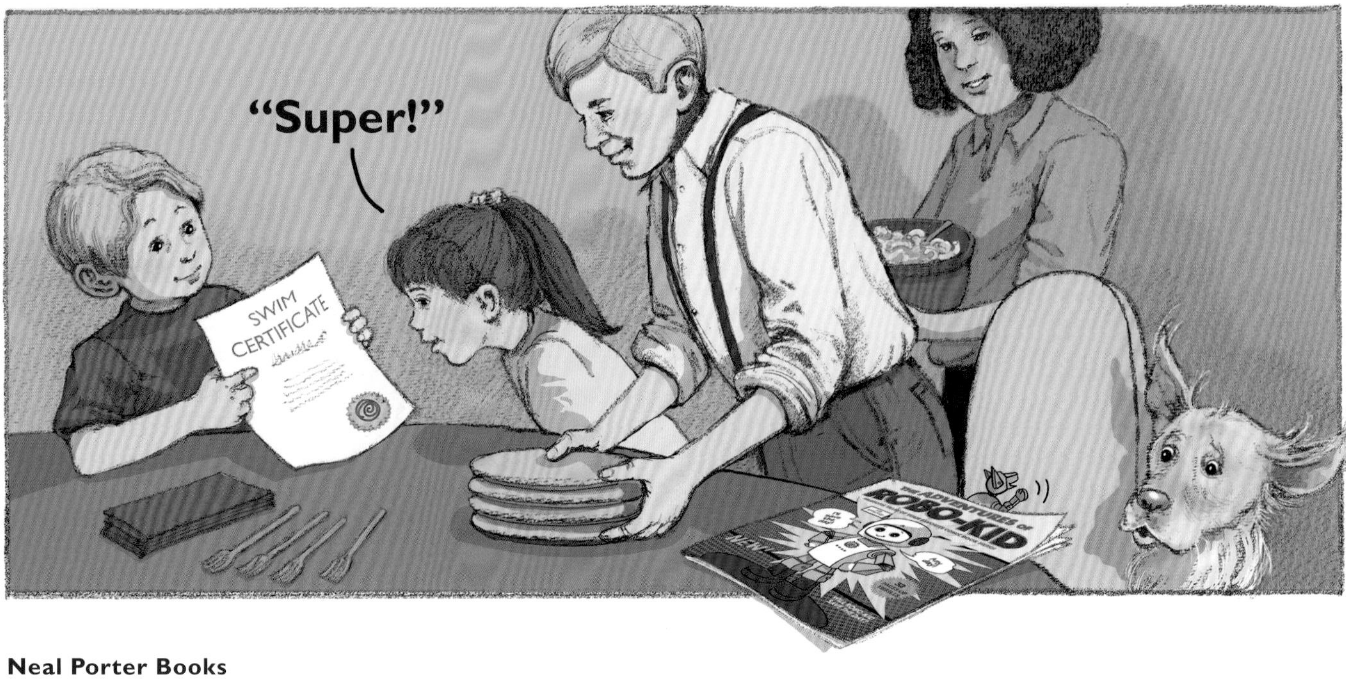
"Super!"
SWIM CERTIFICATE
ROBO-KID

**Neal Porter Books**



Printed and bound in February 2022 at C&C Offset, Shenzhen, China.

The artwork for this book was created with charcoal pencil and enhanced in Photoshop.

www.holidayhouse.com

First Edition

10 9 8 7 6 5 4 3 2 1

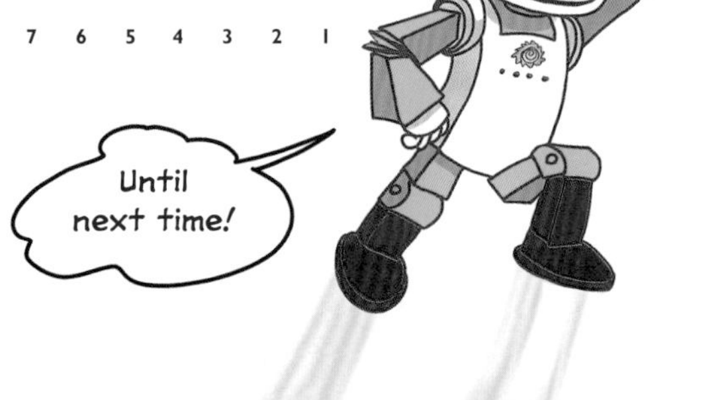
Until next time!

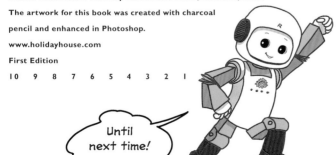

Library of Congress Cataloging-in-Publication Data

Names: De Groat, Diane, author, illustrator.

Title: The adventures of Robo-Kid / by Diane deGroat.

Description: First edition. | New York : Holiday House, [2022] | "A Neal Porter book" | Audience: Ages 4 to 8 | Audience: Grades K–1 | Summary: "A boy's favorite superhero climbs out of a comic book and into the real world"— Provided by publisher.

Identifiers: LCCN 2021037882 | ISBN 9780823449767 (hardcover)

Subjects: CYAC: Superheroes—Fiction. | Imagination—Fiction.

Classification: LCC PZ7.D3639 Ad 2022 | DDC [E]—dc23

LC record available at https://lccn.loc.gov/2021037882

ISBN 978-0-8234-4976-7 (hardcover)

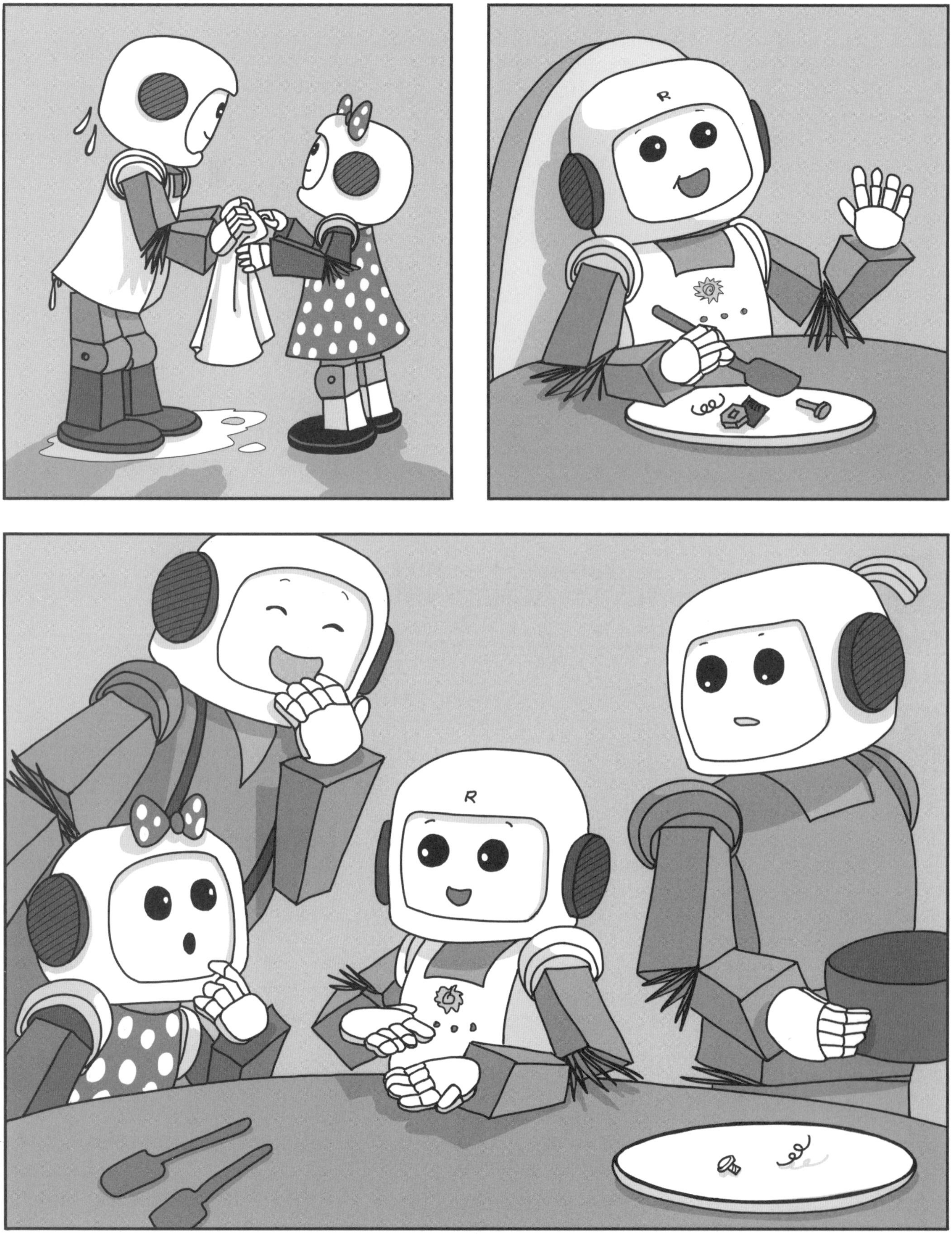